T0154367

Scribe Publications
THE SECRET LIVES OF MEN

Georgia Blain has published novels, a memoir, essays and short stories in Australia and overseas. Her first novel, *Closed for Winter*, was made into a film. She has been shortlisted for numerous awards, including the NSW and SA premier's literary awards, and the Nita B. Kibble Award. Her most recent novels include *Too Close to Home* and *Darkwater*, her first young-adult book.

Also by Georgia Blain

Closed for Winter
Candelo
The Blind Eye
Names for Nothingness
Births Deaths Marriages
Darkwater
Too Close to Home

THE
SECRET
LIVES
OF
MEN

GEORGIA BLAIN

SCRIBE
Melbourne • London

Scribe Publications Pty Ltd
18–20 Edward St, Brunswick, Victoria, Australia 3056
Email: info@scribepub.com.au

First published by Scribe 2013

Typeset in 12/17 pt Adobe Caslon Pro by the publishers
Printed and bound in Australia by Griffin Press

 The paper this book is printed on is certified against the Forest Stewardship Council® Standards. Griffin Press holds FSC chain of custody certification SGS-COC-005088. FSC promotes environmentally responsible, socially beneficial and economically viable management of the world's forests.

These stories first appeared, often in slightly different forms, in the following publications: 'The Secret Lives of Men', *Review of Australian Fiction*; 'Enlarged + Heart + Child', *Griffith REVIEW*; 'Intelligence Quotient', *Meanjin* and *The Best Australian Stories 2009* (Black Inc., 2009); 'The Other Side of the River', *New Australian Stories* (Scribe, 2009); 'Mirrored', *10 Short Stories You Must Read in 2010* (Australia Council for the Arts, 2010); 'Her Boredom Trick', *Griffith REVIEW*; 'Flyover', *New Australian Stories 2* (Scribe, 2010).

National Library of Australia
Cataloguing-in-Publication data

Blain, Georgia.

The Secret Lives of Men.

9781922070357 (pbk.)

A823.4

www.scribepublications.com.au

Contents

THE SECRET LIVES OF MEN   1

ENLARGED + HEART + CHILD   21

INTELLIGENCE QUOTIENT   33

JUST A WEDDING   53

THE BAD DOG PARK   67

BIG DREAMS   89

THE OTHER SIDE OF THE RIVER   109

ESCAPE   125

NORTH FROM SOUTH   149

MIRRORED   167

MURRAMARANG   189

HER BOREDOM TRICK   205

FLYOVER   227

The Secret Lives of Men

We always knew the locals hated us. They stayed in the corner of the pub, all wearing tight black jeans, ripple-soled boots and flannel shirts despite the heat. We stole the occasional glance at them, too scared to let our gaze linger, but they never turned our way; their refusal to give us any form of recognition both powerful and disturbing.

We were private-school boys and girls on holiday, drunk on sickly sweet mixers, trying to pretend we were older than we were as we lit St Moritz cigarettes and called out to each other, our voices shrill as we ordered another G and T or Pimm's with lemonade, drinking until we could drink no more, one of us stumbling towards the toilets, nauseated and pale, a sheen of sweat across the skin.

At night it was cold, desert cold beneath a close black sky, stars like frost shimmering above. You could smell the sea at the end of the street, salty, and the pine resin, antiseptic sharp in the swirl of mist that hovered above the town.

When the pub closed, we went down to the beach, running along the cracked pavements, some of us still clutching glasses in our hand, the glow of our cigarettes cutting through the dark. It was the end of school and we wanted only to drink and smoke and, if we were lucky, to have sex with a boy from one of the better schools, one whose father worked in banking or stockbroking and would set him up in a well-paid job after he finished his economics degree.

Alastair Hanson was slightly older, his hair white against his tan, his eyes like cut ice beneath black lashes as he leant forward to light your cigarette. He wore the uniform of all the others, the moleskin jeans, the striped cotton shirt, but he wore it with insouciance (a word we didn't know then) — *panache*, some of us said when we were drunk; *style*, when we were sober — and we all wished we could be with him.

My best friend, Lara, told me his shirts came from Paris, ordered by his French mother from her favourite shop. He had an earring, too, unheard of then. And he drove a powder-blue MG, with his girlfriend, Tiffany Smythe, always next to him, her mouth sulky, her elbow on the door, her gaze distant and bored, as they parked high above Horseshoe Bay to check the surf.

She would have been home that night. She was so

sure in her ability to hold on to Alastair that there was no need for her to come to the pub. She could stay in the family beach house, sprawled on the couch with her group of friends, drinking something more sophisticated, Canadian Club whiskey or champagne, while below the sea pounded against the pink limestone, wearing it away and away and away.

Alastair usually stayed with her. But he had come to town to buy her cigarettes, and I was drunk enough to amuse him with my impersonation of the local fish-and-chip shop owner, my accent broad, each sentence rising at the end as I mimed slapping a piece of flake onto newspaper, ash from my cigarette spilling on top, and then — to my shame — limping painfully over to the cash register to ring up the sale.

I was louder than I should have been, spurred on by my success in not only keeping his attention but also getting him to buy me a drink. And when the girl behind the bar didn't come immediately, I called out to her in my fish-and-chip voice.

She just glared at us, her eyes narrowed, her lips tight.

'You can leave,' she said to me.

I turned, thinking the culprit was behind me.

'No. You.'

'Aw, come on,' everyone complained, enjoying the game now, and drumming their fists on the sticky bar counter, the racket rising while she remained impervious.

'You've got till I count to five.'

There was something in the timbre of her voice, a sharp edge that was enough to still the crowd, but only for an instant. Johnny Liddell was on the stool, kneeling precariously, hands clasped in front of him and begging for mercy, while behind him the others hooted and whistled.

'How could a beauty like you be so cruel,' he told her, and stood, wobbling as he unbuttoned his fly, promising her a bit of heaven like she'd never known before.

The stool crashed to the ground as the tallest of the local boys rose. I don't even remember what he looked like, or what he said, but I know we were scared and excited and too drunk to assess whether we were in any real danger. Someone shouted *fight fight* and we spilt onto the street, the night air like a brisk slap, seagulls wheeling overhead, ghostly white in the darkness.

It was Johnny they wanted. As he ran up the main street, brawls began to break out: the sickening thud of a punch, the shatter of a glass, a scream. Alastair grabbed me by the arm, and I followed him to his car, with no time to even realise that I was getting into that powder-blue MG, alone next to him, and we sped up the road, past the group of locals who were fast gaining on Johnny, the roar of the engine thrilling.

'Get in,' Alastair yelled, pulling over to let Johnny leap into the back seat behind us.

'Fuck me,' Johnny shouted, and then, to the group of locals who had almost caught him, 'Fuck you.'

And lurching forward, we took off towards the beach, all of us screaming, voices raised to the sky and the ocean and the wind and one another.

I remember nothing else.

I heard about Alastair's death purely by chance. It was Lara's younger sister, Jane, who told me, awkward as she asked whether I'd come back for the funeral, her two boys pulling at her skirt, one whining that he wanted to go home, the other rifling the chocolate bars placed low beneath the counter.

I hadn't. But then I had lost touch with everyone when I left to live in London.

'It was completely sudden. An aneurysm.'

He had two daughters, apparently, and a Swedish wife who had helped him set up his antiques import business.

'I can understand you didn't stay in contact,' she said, uncomfortable now. 'It would have been hard.'

I didn't say anything.

'To be reminded.'

I could see she regretted those last words, and she stumbled awkwardly into telling me once again how well I looked, and how much she loved my dress; I was so lucky to have access to all that London fashion.

I asked her if she knew when the funeral was, and she seemed even more embarrassed. 'It's been.' One of her boys began to scream, a piercing sound. 'Just yesterday.'

'I wish I'd known.'

She touched my arm gently, trying to ignore the sounds of her son, but as the screaming increased in intensity, she said she'd better get him home for his nap. 'He's impossible without it.' She scooped him up, using one free arm to pull at the other boy as she told him it was time to leave. 'I'm so sorry you had to hear like this.'

I could see she wished she knew what to say, despite realising there was no simple phrase capable of smoothing all that had passed.

It had been ten years since I had left this city (I always feel I am lying when I call it that — it is closer to a town), and I had only returned three times, dreading the summer days, dry and gaspingly hot; a place where you could hang a T-shirt on the line and within five minutes it would be stiff like cardboard, the air a fan-forced oven, indiscriminatingly pitiless.

My mother still lived in our house, low in the foothills, the grass always burnt to a crisp and the flowering eucalypts a lurid display of fuchsia, orange, crimson and lemon. There'd been no rain for months, and the native animals would come in from the surrounding bush to drink from the dog's bowl, only to expire, parched, frightened and panting in what little cool they could find. My mother showed me the graves she'd dug, smooth mounds of dry earth under the scrappy shade of the ironbarks.

It was disgusting, she said. The world burning to

death, and corporations worried only about increasing their profits.

In the last decade she had changed. Once a housewife who had helped out at school fundraisers and taken care of all my father's needs with a certain sharp-tongued bitterness, she'd cut ties with all the parents of our school friends and joined a volunteer group to help refugees in detention centres. She ran free English classes from the lounge room, teaching people who'd been released into the community. With the curtains drawn against the daylight, and the slow repetition of words soothing in the heat, this was when she seemed most at ease, calm and content.

'I trained as a teacher,' she once told me. 'And then I wasted years cooking meals for all of you, cleaning, keeping your father happy, worrying whether you were all happy.' She sighed. 'And now I have so little time.'

She disapproved of my older brother, a stockbroker who had made his fortune and lived in an expat compound in the lush hills behind Hong Kong.

As for me, I knew she still worried about my life, although she did her best to keep this to herself. Over the last five years, as I had found a house to live in, friends, and enough work as a graphic designer to keep me busy, her anxiety had lessened a little. I no longer caught her watching me, brows furrowed, tension across her forehead, the lines dissolving as I met her gaze and asked her to give it a rest. 'I'm fine,' I would always say.

When I returned from the delicatessen, green cloth bags filled with organic vegetables and spelt bread, she was on the telephone, organising a visit to the detention centre with her good friend, a nun.

I made us both lunch, and we ate in silence in the cool of the kitchen, the radio on, a quiet hum behind us.

'This house is too big for me,' she said.

My mother often made pronouncements like this, comments that required no answer. Her glasses were off, and her eyes were a pale wash of blue. Her skin was like tissue, and her hands were now too knotted with arthritis to wear her wedding ring.

We had spent a lot of time together right after the accident. Both my legs were broken, and I had been confined, unable to start university as I had planned, too out of place in the world to feel the disappointment I would otherwise have felt at watching all my friends move into this next phase of life.

'Did you hear he died?' I asked her.

The music on the radio heralded the ABC news bulletin, a tune so familiar and yet one I could never hum if I were asked to.

'Alastair, that is.'

She put her sandwich down. 'I thought you meant the other one,' she said. 'The one in the home.'

I shook my head. 'I would have gone to his funeral if I'd known. I would've liked to have said goodbye.'

Her response was immediate. 'You lost touch for

good reason.' She kept her eyes fixed on me. 'Was it an overdose?'

I told her it wasn't. 'He became respectable.' And I smiled. 'A wife, daughters, an antique business.'

I hadn't imagined he would stay in this town, let alone find a place for himself here.

My mother reached for my hand. Her touch was cool and dry, her hold steady, but her voice was — for her — surprisingly frail. 'I didn't hate him, you know. I just didn't like what you were doing to each other. It was a downward spiral of self-disgust and you can't watch your child do that. You can't.' She stroked my hair back from my face. 'You'd been through enough. You had to forgive yourselves, and you weren't going to do that together.'

I was alone in the garden when I first saw Alastair after the accident. I opened my eyes to find him standing above me, his body blocking the warmth of the winter sun.

'Jesus.' Startled, I sat upright, my book falling to the ground, pages bent back, cover facing up.

My mother had wheeled me out with a novel, and a blanket over my knees, but I had just stared across the lawn and down to the street, until finally I'd dozed off, the painkillers I was taking for the backaches too strong to resist.

He apologised for shocking me. Unable to meet my gaze, he said he hadn't wanted to disturb me, he'd just wanted to see me. 'I came to the hospital. But you were asleep.' He picked up the book and placed it carefully on my lap.

'Well, here I am.' I pointed at my legs, both in casts. And then, because I hadn't meant to be so harsh, I told him that they would be coming off soon, that I would be out of the wheelchair and walking. 'It's not like I'm going to be a cripple or anything. They're just broken.'

Reaching down, his hair falling across his eyes, he touched the hard white surface of the plaster. The sensation was strange, seeing his fingers run down my leg but not feeling a thing, and I hadn't meant to start crying. I can only assume it was the drugs I was on, but I did cry, the tears hot and shameful, and I wiped them away as he knelt beside me, hands shaking, and lit a cigarette.

'Here.' He put it in my mouth, and I drew back deeply, exhaling as I told him my arms still worked, I could hold it myself. He took one more drag and passed the cigarette to me.

'Do they know you're here?' I asked him.

They didn't.

Eyes like pewter in the winter light, hair like flax. I was dosed up on codeine and god knows what else, and I ran my fingers through the fall of his fringe as he sat there, also smoking, his hands still shaking. Then, grinding the cigarette into the dirt, he stood up.

'Come with me,' he said.

I didn't know what he meant.

'Let's just go somewhere.'

'I can't,' I said. 'I can't go anywhere.' I wasn't sure what kind of game he was playing with me, or if I was even dreaming his presence, and as he knelt down close, I pushed at him, not strong enough to have any effect, all of me heavy and slow and confused. I realised we were both crying now and we started kissing, his hands on my breasts, his hair silky against my skin as he said he just wanted to wheel me down the street, that was all, away from here, before my parents came out.

'Okay,' I whispered. 'Okay.'

He took me out of our gate and along the footpath towards the gully reserve, a place I had played in as a child, years ago when I hung out with the other kids in our neighbourhood, building bridges over what used to be a creek, and climbing trees, silvery branches trembling beneath our weight.

We stopped behind the boulders, hidden from the road, and I wanted to go back, it had all been too much after weeks of being confined at home, but as I opened my mouth to speak he began to talk.

'I saw him,' he said, and it took me a moment before I realised he was referring to Johnny. He was rolling a joint, staring at the paper between his fingers, turning it tighter and tighter. 'My dad took me there. He left me sitting with him for an hour.' He glanced up at the tracing of branches and leaves, a knot of limbs against the sky, and then down to the ground, the twigs and gumnuts and bark at our feet.

GEORGIA BLAIN

'He just lies in his bed, head to one side, and it's not him.'

I could feel an ant crawling across my wrist and I flicked it away.

'Can you take me home?' I asked, or at least I thought I did, but it seemed no sound would come out, so instead I touched his face, bringing him towards me, his mouth on mine again.

'Oh god,' I said, because the weight of him hurt. He traced the tips of his fingers down my shirt, unbuttoning it now, and I wondered what the fuck we were doing, out here, me in the wheelchair, him slowly undressing me, kissing my breast, his mouth on my nipples, his hands down my skirt now, and I didn't know what I felt or wanted or needed, I just didn't want Alastair to speak of Johnny. I took his belt in my hands, undoing it, while overhead a crow watched us, eyes glittering, and ants crawled through the dirt and a lizard flicked across the rocks behind us and we tried so hard to lose ourselves.

When he took me home, my mother was in the garden, furious with me for not telling her, angry with him for being so irresponsible, *again*; and she knew she was sticking the knife in, she knew she was hurting him.

He ignored her. Bending down to kiss me, he whispered that he would be back. 'Soon,' he promised.

And he was. No matter how much my parents protested. He came each day, wheeling me down to the gully where we fucked and drank, the fallen leaves and twigs tangled in the sleeves of my coat and in my hair, the smell of the dope thick in my clothes and the scent of him buried deep in my skin.

'Why don't you like him?' I once shouted at my mother. 'He was just trying to get us away from the fight. He was trying to do the right thing.'

As soon as I was out of the wheelchair, I stopped coming home, staying with him in the flat his parents had bought, living off his money, both of us out all night, in the few clubs and bars open late, or at parties held by people we didn't know, where we were the wild entertainment, the ones who had gone off the rails, scary and too much for this place.

'You're a mess,' Lara once told me angrily in a pub, and I could only sneer at her, a strange cocktail of shame and superiority coursing in my veins.

But sometimes, when we would sleep in, sweaty and restless in each other's arms, I would hate what we had become. I would wake in the early afternoon and see us both in that sharp light, Alastair still beautiful, eyes closed, skin pale gold, and I would wish that I was someone else.

I would like to say I was the one who decided it was time to leave. But that wasn't how it went. He left me. Dragging himself with an extraordinary will away from the inertia and mess of our life together, weeping each time I begged him to come back, he eventually checked himself into a private rehab clinic in Melbourne.

And there I was. Alone.

Standing outside Alastair's empty flat, I saw myself reflected in the glass door to the building. Lank hair, eyes wide and scared, body too thin, acne across my chin, unsteady on platform shoes with scuffed plastic straps.

I called my mother and she came and picked me up.

Driving home, with the little I owned on the back seat, she told me she would always be there for me, but the time had come to take responsibility for myself.

'I love you,' she said.

I didn't reply.

Outside the window I could see the streets of the town I despised, the shadow of my own face layered over the roads and houses and gardens.

'It's not like you were driving,' she continued, nervous because we never talked about the accident. 'I mean, he had every reason — after what happened to that poor boy. But you were just a passenger.'

Keeping my eyes on the window, I tried not to listen. *I'm not blameless.* I mouthed the words, watching the shape of my mouth.

I'd had them all in stitches that night in the pub. The fish-and-chip lady, accent broad, limp pronounced, stupid, worthless and ugly. And I had thought I was so funny. Until everything began to spiral, wild, fast and completely out of control.

On the day before my flight back to London, I borrowed my mother's car, telling her I wanted to drive through the hills. I knew she was teaching and wouldn't join me. She handed me the keys, asking me when I'd be back, and I promised it would be in time for dinner, aware this would be our last meal together for some time.

The day was cooler, peppery eucalypts and the sweetness of melted tar rich beneath the crisp air. I hadn't come this way for years, not since I was at school and on a camp that involved chill morning swims, bush walks and tasteless food dumped onto our tin plates. Sneaking out at night, we would sit beneath the pale stars, the frost of our breath merging with the smoke from our smuggled cigarettes, our giggles hushed as we gossiped and bickered, telling lies about who we liked and who we didn't.

As I passed through one-street towns, sandstone buildings crumbling into the hills, some set up for tourists, others almost deserted, I knew where I was headed, although I wasn't sure of what I intended to do when I arrived.

I had found the address the evening after I'd heard of his death. He had a shop in one of the larger towns on the way to the Coorong, a place where people came to buy antiques on a lazy Sunday excursion. The website showed off a collection of Danish and Swedish furniture, sourced on regular trips back to Scandinavia, and I'd searched through the images, hoping to find a picture of him, perhaps even accidentally captured as his wife photographed a new piece in a back corner. But there was nothing.

Because it was a weekday, and the school holidays were over, the main street was empty. Wide verandahs shielded the footpath from the increasing heat of the sun, and nearly every shop was closed, only opening for business when the Saturday and Sunday visitors came. I was anxious that his would be shut, too, yet there was also a part of me hoping to find it locked up, so I could simply peer through the windows, feel disappointed and drive home. And at first, this was how it seemed to be, the doors pulled to, a lack of light inside indicating emptiness, but as I pressed my nose to the glass, I saw a woman at a desk, her face hidden by a sweep of auburn hair.

She looked up as I pushed on the door, waving her arm to indicate that no, they were closed, she was sorry — but it was too late, I had already stepped inside and I, too, was apologising as she stood, tall and elegant in a pale blue cotton dress.

'I thought I had locked the door,' she said.

I held out my hand towards her, saying that I hadn't come to buy, I was in fact an old friend of Alastair's. As I uttered my name, her eyes widened in recognition.

I told her I'd been overseas for some time now, I only just heard of his death the other day, quite by accident.

'I was so sorry,' I said. 'It must have been a terrible shock.'

She nodded, still not speaking, and I continued in a rush of words, saying that I wished I'd been able to go to the funeral, to have marked his passing in some way, and that was perhaps why I had driven down here, to try to somehow reconnect with him; and I wondered if I should head out the door and leave her, because I felt foolish and intrusive.

She turned the key in the lock and asked if I wanted to sit, perhaps have a drink.

'I was just trying to cancel the last order he made, but he kept such terrible notes.' She led me through to the kitchen at the back of the shop. 'I want to close up, to get back home, you see. I don't want to live here anymore.' She glanced out the window at the wide, empty street.

I told her I was surprised that Alastair had chosen this place to settle.

'He didn't want to be in town,' she explained. 'Near all the people who knew him and what had happened.'

'Why didn't he leave? Live in another city or country?'

The room was large, with white walls, transom windows to let in light and air, a high wooden ceiling and heavy stone flaggings on the floor. She put a jug of iced water on the table between us and sat across from me, saying she often asked him that question herself.

'But I never had an answer.' Her face was tired. 'And then when he died, I finally got it.'

Outside I could hear a mother talking to her child, and from across the road the turn of a car engine and the gunning of an accelerator, motor throbbing in the noon stillness.

'Every Tuesday he would drive to the city,' she continued. 'He told me he had an NA meeting he liked to go to. And I never presumed otherwise. But it wasn't the truth.' She poured us both a glass of water from the jug.

Her voice was quiet when she spoke again. 'They called me when he died. He had just left the home, and was outside in the garden, walking towards his car. He collapsed on the pavement. It was instant.'

I didn't understand.

'He never went to NA meetings. He went there. Each Tuesday, to visit him.'

I stared up at the windows, the chain heavy and well oiled, and beyond the glass, a slice of sky, flat, blue and hard.

'They said he came at the same time every week and sat with him for an hour. Sometimes he read to him; other times he just stayed by his side and held his hand.'

A clock in the showroom struck the hour, sonorous and slow. 'How long?' I asked her.

'Since the accident,' she said. 'Most weeks. Apparently he had become the only visitor. The mother and father died about two years ago, and no one else came.' She looked down at the table. 'It's an awful fate, to be left like that. Completely alone.'

I wondered at all the times he would have gone there in the brief period we were together.

'I never knew,' I said.

Her eyes were kind. 'Nor did I.'

'He was ashamed.' I studied the worn sandstone at our feet, uneven and pale. 'He thought it was his fault. But Johnny wasn't sitting in the car properly and I —' There were so many factors. There always are. I glanced up at her. 'Alastair walked out of there without any injury and he never forgave himself.'

'I think he did,' she said.

Later, as I drove home across the hills with the afternoon light holding back the darkness, I wondered whether she was right.

She had shown me photographs of him and their two daughters, pictures on her phone and prints that hung in the back rooms where they lived. He was as beautiful as he had always been, tall and slender, skin like honey. Their girls were called Ingrid and Christina, both in school, one like him and one like her. He was a good father, she had said, gentle and attentive, and she had started crying then, quickly brushing away her tears as soon as they fell.

At the doorway, I told her I was glad I had come, and I gave her my address in London, although I knew it was unlikely she would ever contact me. As she wrote it down, I took in the house behind her one more time, his coat in the hall, and beneath that his boots, his bag at the bottom of the stairs, traces of him everywhere, a life that still lingered, held on to by those who were left behind.

$\mathcal{E}$nlarged + $\mathcal{H}$eart + $\mathcal{C}$hild

Wednesday is dog day. Or dog afternoon, to be more precise. In fact, it's only a twenty-minute distraction, but when you have so little to cling to, you take what you can get.

This week Shelly and Annie are dressed in their PAT volunteer tracksuits, and they have brought both the dogs to the children's hospital. Shelly has Max, a quiet brown labrador, and Annie has Lulu, the poodle. Leone and Ruby have seen them both before, and it's depressing to count back and realise they've now been in ward 3C South for four dog days, which equals four weeks, which is close enough to a month — a length of time too sad to countenance.

Ruby is sitting up next to her bed, cheeks still a high pink from the fever that is only just starting to abate. She takes Leone's hand as soon as she notices Lulu just outside the ward entrance — Lulu is her favourite, and she wants Leone to stay and watch Lulu's tricks again, rather than going to get a cool drink from the fridge.

'Who's met Lulu before?' Annie asks, and Ruby is the only one in the ward to raise her hand.

The others are all new. Bed 4 came in last night and has complained continuously, shouting at her parents not to touch her, to get her food, no she doesn't want that, why can't she go home, why did this have to happen to her, why not someone else?

Ruby's eyes widen with each outburst, and she turns her head so that only Leone can see her mouth the words: *She's got a broken arm, that's all.*

Leone would like to tell the girl to shut the fuck up, but of course she doesn't, and each time Bed 4's mother apologises for her daughter's behaviour, Leone is appropriately sympathetic.

Now, as Annie brings Lulu right into the centre of the ward, Bed 4 tells her to stay away, she doesn't like dogs, keep her back; and her mother is once again saying how sorry she is, her daughter is just scared.

'She's only a little poodle,' her mother tries.

Bed 4 is having none of it. 'I don't want her near me.'

Bed 1, opposite Ruby, has been lying flat on her back since she came up from surgery two days ago. Cerebral palsy and an operation on her knees to try to keep her out of a wheelchair. Her dad sits by her side, doing the crossword, rousing his daughter from her morphine haze to see the dogs.

'She does tricks,' Ruby explains, more to the father than Bed 1 because Bed 1 has not yet been able to lift her head and talk.

He is the joking type and he ruffles his daughter's hair. 'Tricks, hey?' He raises an eyebrow. 'Can she read and write?'

Ruby shakes her head.

'Not interested then.' He winks and folds the paper.

Bed 2 is empty and Bed 3 has the curtains drawn. This morning there were social workers with her, and their talk was hushed but still loud enough to catch certain words. An overdose. Second attempt.

There is weariness in the mother's voice each time her daughter begs to be allowed to go home.

'You hate me,' Bed 3 cries out. 'You don't want me to come back.'

Leone knows Ruby listens to it all, the drama disturbing and better than any of the young-adult books she has been trying to read in between bouts of fever.

Lulu the poodle waits patiently in the middle of the ward for Max to do his rounds. Max has no tricks: he is just a gentle labrador, with dark eyes and a thick chocolate-brown coat. He wags his tail, back sunk low as he makes his way over to where Ruby sits, eager to run her hands through his hair. She reaches out, her arm too thin now, the veins blue against the white of her skin, and sinks her fingers into the warmth of his fur. Max rests his head in her lap, and Ruby breathes in deeply.

Leone kneels by her side.

'He's beautiful, isn't he?' Leone whispers, not quite trusting herself to talk.

Every day for the last four weeks, Leone and Jacob have texted photos of Ruby's dog to her. He is called Harry, and he is large and hairy, ridiculous in the outfits that they dress him in for the daily shoot. Jacob borrowed a child's stethoscope and sent in a picture of Dr Harry; Leone has draped pink cloth over his head, transforming him into Nurse Harry; on other days they leave him just as he is and label their messages Harry In The Raw.

They have plotted sneaking him into the hospital carpark and getting Ruby down there, but she always refuses, scared he will knock her over in his enthusiasm, or pull her cannula out.

'I'll wait,' she tells them.

And that's what she's been doing.

When the GP first told them that Ruby had an enlarged heart, Leone did what she knew she shouldn't. She went straight home and googled: *enlarged + heart + child*. The results were alarming.

The next day, the diagnosis was made by the specialist. Pericarditis, or the collection of excessive fluid between the two walls that surround the chambers. Pictures of Ruby's heart were shown to them on a computer screen. Leone held her breath as she watched it beat beautifully, the valve opening and closing, opening and closing, with a steady rhythm. The doctor examined it from each angle, capturing shots every few seconds. There were times when the heart was like a gorilla's nose, Leone thought, black and wet, the nostrils breathing in and out.

The doctor pointed out the fluid, and the build-up of fibrous strands, like jellyfish tentacles. The walls had thickened. He told them it was surprising the function appeared perfectly normal.

'The danger is the movement of the heart will be constricted,' he explained. 'And that's why we need to operate.'

'I must have a very strong heart,' Ruby said after he left.

Leone could only nod.

That night, Ruby was wheeled into theatre. Jacob stayed with her as she went under. Leone couldn't do it.

He joined Leone in the windowless waiting room off intensive care soon after, his face pale. 'It was like watching her die,' he said.

She held his hand as his shoulders heaved, and together they waited.

The surgery went well. An hour later Ruby was brought into intensive care, bleary and complaining about the oxygen mask, her skin waxy, and her hair tangled around her face.

'I didn't feel a thing,' she told them, before lapsing once again into a deep sleep.

Four weeks later and they are still here.

Leone looks at Ruby now, Max's head resting in her lap, and she wonders how much longer they can bear this unexplained deterioration. When she washes her in the shower, she can see each bone, her skeletal frame delicate like a bird's, pressing against her taut skin.

Everyone had thought she would be heading home within a fortnight of surgery, but a week after the operation, the fevers began. Two or three a day, each reaching forty or forty-one degrees, and no reason to be found. There were teams of doctors, and they gave her new tests all the time — the wall of her heart, fluid from her lungs, blood from her veins, sputum and urine, all extracted and analysed.

Her body never gave a clue.

'A fever can only last so long,' one of the nurses said, 'before another symptom appears.'

And so they continued to wait and see, not knowing what it was that they were waiting for, what they were expecting to see, while Ruby grew weaker, and the days of hospital routine ground the three of them down into splinters and grit, pieces that no longer held together.

Max the labrador thumps his tail against the floor as Ruby scratches behind his ears.

'He likes you,' Shelly tells her.

Shelly is a grey-haired, tough old woman, who only has time for animals and children, and even that is limited. She lets Ruby pat Max a little longer and then, conscious that the clock is ticking, she leads him over to Bed 1.

'Look, sweetheart.' The father tries to help his daughter raise herself slightly, but she can't.

Shelly offers to put Max up on the bed.

'Is he allowed?' Ruby asks Leone, in a very quiet whisper.

She shrugs and tells her that he must be.

Shelly lays a towel down and taps the side of the bed. Max is up, his leap quick and light, and then he lies, close against the girl's body as she utters a tiny, and very drugged, laugh.

'Oh,' she croaks to her father, as she runs a hand down Max's fur.

And they leave him there as Lulu gets ready for her turn.

Annie is friendlier than Shelly. Small and spry with brilliant blue eyes, she enjoys showing Lulu off.

The curtains around Bed 3 are pulled back, and the mother sits perched on the edge of the mattress while her daughter lies behind her, curled into a ball. She doesn't even attempt to rouse her or encourage her to enjoy the show. She just stares blankly as Lulu begins to prance on her hind legs, delicate like a ballerina. Ridiculous, in fact.

'Now backwards.' Annie clicks her fingers, and Lulu is down on all fours, walking the wrong way, round and round in a circle.

'How does she know how to do that?' Ruby asks, as she asks every week.

Next is the skateboard trick, Ruby's favourite. She sits forward in the purple vinyl hospital chair, and Leone brushes her lank hair back behind her ears. It's been a few days since she's been able to get her in the shower. The times between fevers are becoming shorter, and she is always tired now.

'Can't I just sit?' Ruby usually asks, and most of the time Leone gives way, sponging her with a wipe from the storeroom.

Annie puts a skateboard down on the floor and clicks her fingers.

Bed 3 uncurls, lean legs in tight jeans, her oversize T-shirt doing nothing to hide how thin her body is. She tries to close the curtain, but her mother has it firm in her grasp.

'I want to shut it,' Bed 3 complains.

Leone can see the white of the mother's knuckles as she clutches the nylon and mutters to her daughter. They will pull it off the railing, Leone thinks.

Lulu is on the board now, and she and Ruby and even Bed 4 (who has been surprisingly silent, since she made it clear she didn't want a dog near her) are all staring at her, but they are also attuned to the conflict opposite, recognising that the show could suddenly move to a different stage.

'Close it,' Bed 3 insists, while Lulu does her best, one leg down on the lino floor, pushing herself along with bright, perky dexterity — round and round she goes —

but no one is really paying attention.

The mother does not move.

'I want to go home. I don't want to be here.'

Oh god, Leone thinks.

'Why won't you let me leave?'

The clasp on Lulu's collar tinkles as she stands on her hind legs. The board wobbles, but she doesn't topple.

'I don't want to watch a poodle.' Bed 3's voice is close to a shout, and they cannot pretend not to hear.

Leone tries to catch the mother's eye and grimace in sympathy, but she remains with her gaze fixed on the floor.

Bed 3 swings her legs down and stands up, all bones, her mousy hair hiding her face. Ruby reaches for Leone's hand, anxious, her fingers frail and slightly sweaty, as Lulu lowers herself back onto all fours. She is waiting for the applause. There is none.

'I don't care about a fucking poodle.' Bed 3 takes her mother's shoulders in her hands, wanting her mother to face her. 'Can't you hear me? I don't care about a fucking poodle.'

It's all Leone can do not to join her, not to say, *None of us care about a fucking poodle, all of us want to get out of here, god in heaven help us*, but she just holds Ruby's hand tight and tells her it will be okay, it's nothing to worry about, nothing at all.

The male nurse comes in and takes Bed 3 by the arm, trying to calm her down, soothing her, as the mother walks out of the ward.

Annie packs up Lulu and the board, and Shelly clicks her fingers to Max, who leaps down, his job done.

Opposite, the father of Bed 1 glances up from his crossword. His daughter reaches for her morphine button, and he kisses her on the forehead.

'Think we could all do with a go of that,' he says.

And Leone tries to smile.

Later, in the evening, as Leone sits at home alone, she weeps. This is what she does most nights, sometimes as soon as she gets inside the front door to the empty house, a meal left by a friend on the kitchen table, everything clean and tidy; other times not until the depths of the night, when she wakes with a start, aware that her daughter and her partner are not there with her, but are in a ward under fluorescent lights, the television on, Jacob sponging Ruby's forehead, cooling her in the hope that she will sleep.

On the floor of the kitchen, Leone holds her knees to her chest and she is terrified.

She no longer knows what to google. Unexplained fever, prolonged temperature, post-operative infections, pericarditis + complications — none of them gives her the answer she desperately wants to the question she hardly dares ask: *Will it be alright?*

And so she cries, all of her sick with fear, each nerve ending spliced and raw, the bile rising as she rocks backwards and forwards, weeping, unable to stop until Harry the dog slinks over, anxious and unsure of what to do.

He noses her, nudging and whimpering, forcing her to stretch her legs out. He is a large dog, the size of an alsatian, but he tries to curl up, smaller than Lulu, desperate to keep his entire body on her lap, and she holds him tight until she can breathe without sobbing, until she is still.

It is late and she hasn't sent the picture to Ruby.

Wiping at her eyes, she gets up, exhausted. There is nothing immediately at hand, no outfit she can think of that will work, and she feels so very tired, but she knows Ruby likes the dress-up photographs best.

Then she sees it, Ruby's football scarf hanging on a hook in the kitchen, and in her room there is the jersey that she made Jacob buy her last season.

Harry the Brownlow Medallist. She hangs a medal around his neck to complete the look and then texts it off. Ruby will like it, and tomorrow is Thursday, Leone realises, football day, when the players come to hand out plastic crap and have their photos taken with the sick kids. Not even vaguely entertaining the first time round, but she knows that when she goes into the ward in the morning, she will tell Ruby that the Swans or Tigers or Eels are coming in today, and they will both try to be excited, grateful for the team bag and drink bottle, the autographs and teddy bears dressed in team colours. As soon as the players leave, Leone will put all the junk in a bag, ready to bring home, where it will wait, unpacked, in the corner of Ruby's room.

Intelligence Quotient

Just before I turned forty, my mother, who was the only other member of my family still alive, died from a stroke. She left me a small amount of money, enough for a deposit on a semi in a suburb not too far from the city, a place where the streets were hilly and treeless, and the houses that hadn't been knocked down to build huge brick villas remained unrenovated.

I'd never had my own place, nor had I lived by myself, and when I first received the key, I held it tight, hesitant about putting it on the ring with the others. And then I slotted it through the steel loop, its bright, shiny newness marking it out as different from the rest.

I had no work at the time, so I stacked most of the little furniture I owned into one room and began to remove the remnants of the lives that had been lived here before me. I lifted carpets weighed down by years of dust;

I pulled back linoleum, finding faded patterns of flowers on tiles that were cracked with age. I scrubbed down walls and painted. I listened to the radio as I worked, hours of music and talk that wafted over me as the days passed.

One morning, when I was out on the street putting an undercoat on the front fence, a car pulled over, the engine rattling as it idled. A woman reached across the passenger seat and wound down the window.

'I heard you were in the neighbourhood.' Her blonde hair was pulled back in a scrappy ponytail and her tanned skin was lined. As she pushed her sunglasses up on her head, I could see that her eyes were pale green, a startling colour beneath lashes that were brittle with clumps of mascara. 'You don't remember me.'

Balancing the paintbrush on the edge of the can, I took a step towards the car, shaking my head as I did so. 'I'm sorry.' At first I'd thought she might have recognised me from one of the occasional ads I'd done. Most of these were now old repeats that rarely aired, but I'd recently played a teller in a bank commercial and I'd seen it only the other night.

'It's Juliette.' She rested her hand on the top of the open window, a ring on each of her fingers, three or four heavy silver bangles jangling on her wrist. 'Juliette Acott.'

I wiped my hair from my forehead, breathing in the acrid paint on my skin.

'I used to babysit you.'

I shaded my eyes from the glare. 'Really?' And I leant a little closer.

'The Acott sisters. There were five of us. You sometimes played with Susie, my youngest sister.'

I could sense something tugging at the thick shroud that always cloaked the past: a house on the corner, the sandstone wall covered in jasmine, and Juliette — was it her sunbaking in our garden and smoking cigarettes, while she supposedly looked after us?

'How extraordinary,' I said. 'Do you live around here, too?'

She did. Up the road and next to Alison, the only person I knew in the neighbourhood.

'No, I didn't just recognise you,' she explained as I began to ask how she'd known it was me. 'Although I read about that film you made, and told people that I used to babysit you.' Her voice was husky, deep and cracked.

I asked her how Susie was, and Juliette told me she was living in New York. 'An investment banker, earning a shitload of money.'

'And the others?'

'All doing their thing,' she said, and then, inevitably: 'Your brother? Eddie?'

'He died,' and, because I thought she would probably ask me how, I had to elaborate. 'Killed himself, actually.'

'Jesus,' she said. 'Wouldn't have picked it.' She stared at me with those pale eyes. 'You always seemed the one headed for trouble.'

I was uncertain as to how to respond.

'Do you want to come in?' I eventually asked, glancing down at the paint tin and the half-finished fence.

She'd already pulled the car over and switched off the engine. 'I'll make us a cup of tea.' As she stepped out into the bright glare of the day, I searched for something familiar, a reminder of the girl she'd once been. She was tall and strong, her jeans close-fitting, and her cotton shirt a delicate print of soft blues and crimsons. The fine bones in her face and the remarkable colour of her eyes marked her out as a one-time beauty.

'Milk in yours?' she asked as she made her way through the open front door.

I watched her disappear down the hallway, and I put the brush in a bucket of water and closed the lid on the paint tin.

When I bought my house, Jono had assumed he was coming with me. I guess I did, too. But as he began to talk about building a studio out the back for home recording, I saw him, standing in my kitchen, surveying it all with plans in his eyes, and I wasn't so sure. I was tired of waiting for him to agree to having a child; of waking in the middle of the night, hollowed out by the realisation that I was kidding myself when I thought he would change his mind. I would watch him sleeping, peaceful, and I would hate him.

He was shocked when I told him I was going to live

on my own. He didn't want me to go. We could work it out.

It was hard breaking the habit of trying to believe in him, I confessed to Juliette, surprised at how readily I was talking to her about my life.

Her bangles clanked as she lit a cigarette. 'I've met the type.'

Jono never gave much to the people he supposedly loved. He was the kind of man who's closer to his ex-partners than his current girlfriend, I explained.

'I saw him the other day.' I reached for the milk, smelling it to check it hadn't gone sour. 'He wanted to see a movie together. Afterwards we had dinner. He told me he was with a woman called Sally. Just a casual thing, he said. She wanted a lot more, but he wasn't ready.'

Across the street, a neighbour's cat was lying in the sun, her sleek body stretched out on top of the wall. 'I suddenly realised that was probably how he'd described our relationship to each of his old girlfriends when we were together.'

Juliette was squinting in the brightness of the day. 'Never known a man who was worth it. Sounds like you're better off without him.'

Maybe, I conceded, although I wasn't entirely sure. My desire for a child crippled me at times, particularly now I was completely alone. At least with Jono there'd been some hope, no matter how false. Now I spent a lot of time trying to face the strong likelihood it wouldn't be fulfilled.

'But I like it here,' I said, looking at my house behind me. And I did. After years of drifting from place to place, I felt comfort and relief at this sense of ownership. *I am home*, I would tell myself. *At last, I am home.*

Juliette was a painter. Before that she'd been a cook, a nurse and a childcare worker. There'd been a few men, but none had stayed around. She'd lived by herself in a semi not that dissimilar to mine for the last ten years. 'I'm better off that way.' She laughed throatily. 'People like us' — and I was surprised at how readily she grouped us together — 'we never really learnt how to play the game. You know, not like them.' She waved her arm in a sweeping gesture that took in the rows of streets and houses in a suburb peopled by families. 'But it's not all bad,' she continued, tightening the knot in her hair as it threatened to come loose. 'Swimming against the tide.'

A few days later, I saw her again, out on the street. She was walking briskly down the hill towards the station, one hand clutching a cigarette, the other holding a phone to her ear. As I raised an arm in greeting, she stopped. 'I never said I'd be ready by then,' she told the caller, and held the phone away as she mouthed the words: *Beer, my place tonight?* I could only nod as she returned to her conversation. 'Listen. It's not possible.' She kept walking, without even stopping to see whether I'd agreed to the invitation, dropping her cigarette on the pavement and leaving it smouldering behind her.

That night, Juliette told me she had a great idea for a film. We were sitting in her courtyard, slapping at mosquitoes as they whined close to our ankles and arms. I was only on my second beer but I felt drunk.

'Five sisters.' She tilted her head back, blowing out a thin plume of smoke that was swallowed by the darkness, and took the last swig of ale. 'Arsehole father. Starts with each one of them on her twelfth birthday, until finally, when he gets to the youngest, the other four are all there hiding in her room that night, ready to stop him.'

I didn't know what to say. Looking at her in the glow from the inside lights, I was about to open my mouth and express some puny form of sympathy, when she laughed again.

'It's not my family.' She began to cough. 'Jesus. You remember what my dad was like. Mr Meek and Mild. Wouldn't hurt a fly.'

I didn't. I remembered very little, in fact.

I asked her if she had some photos.

'Somewhere,' she replied. Was I interested in her film idea?

I tried to explain that I didn't work like that. I only ever wrote when it was my own idea; otherwise, I was a director for hire on other people's scripts. If she had written something, I could read it. Alternatively, if she wanted someone to write the story, she'd need to find a screenwriter; they'd have to raise money. As my words amassed, she got up to go to the kitchen.

She brought a couple more beers out, along with half a frozen pizza that had been reheated. I took a slice. She didn't touch it.

'I told Suze about bumping into you again,' she said. 'She remembered you and Eddie doing Mum's IQ test.'

I smiled, the first clear memory falling into place, casting light on others that clung to the edges of our conversation: Susie, Juliette, all the sisters; and that house on the corner, the one I had vaguely recalled with the high stone wall that stopped you from seeing into the garden, although you could still make out the top storey and the slate roof from the street. The bedrooms had been upstairs. Camille and Juliette shared, and then there was Deborah (who had been in Eddie's year at school) and Amanda and, lastly, Susie in a room on her own.

It was Camille who'd looked after us most often. She, too, had blonde hair, loose and silky smooth. When she babysat us during the day, she'd strip down to a string bikini and sunbake lying on her back, and then her side, and then her front, lifting the edges of the crochet to check on the progress of her tan. Sometimes her boyfriend came with her, and Eddie and I would spy on them as his hands worked their way into her bikini bottoms, until she pushed him off and sat up again, leaning across him to reach for her pack of St Moritz cigarettes in the grass.

He would roll joints, carefully spreading a fine line of tobacco and dope along one edge of the paper, rolling it between the thumb and first two fingers of one hand.

'Want some?' he once asked Eddie, who, at a couple of years older than me, was just twelve — almost too old for a babysitter, but because he and I had a tendency to argue, our parents didn't like to leave us alone.

Cross-legged on the emerald-green lawn, Eddie tried to measure up to the adult status that was being offered. Voice cracking as he reached out a hand and told the boyfriend (whose name I couldn't remember) that yeah, sure, a toke'd be good; Eddie didn't dare look at me watching him. Breathing deep, he held the smoke in, holding it, holding it, until unable to bear it any longer, he bent forward, coughing out a choking cloud, while the joint kept burning.

'Don't waste it,' the boyfriend scolded, and I could see Eddie was mortified.

'What about me?' I asked, sure I could do a better job than my brother.

'Like this,' and pinching the end of the joint, Camille's boyfriend drew back, a sharp intake of breath, holding it for a moment, before letting the air out.

Eddie watched.

'I wouldn't give him any more,' Camille half protested, standing slowly. 'And I definitely wouldn't give her any.' We all kept our eyes on her as she walked, tanned and languorous, down to the house, the sunlight cutting through the slender poplars that marked the border between us and next door.

She was the ideal woman, Eddie told me later. He

drew pictures of her, sketches on the back of school notes and in exercise books, line drawings that never quite caught the perfect symmetry of her features. He wrote her name over and over again, scribbling it out as soon as he completed it. He even took a photograph of her, keeping it crumpled under his pillow.

Once, he and his friends had followed her and the other fourth formers to the dank marshy ground under the Gladesville Bridge, where magic mushrooms grew in the clotted dirt near the concrete pylons. Camille discovered Eddie hiding in the sticky asthma weed, and her boyfriend gave him a mushroom to try.

'You didn't,' I said.

Eddie just rolled his eyes, and although I didn't want to ask him what it was like, I wanted to know.

'Amazing.' His fringe fell across his face, and he pushed it aside. 'We took it in turns to kiss her.'

'Who?'

'Camille.'

I knew then he was lying.

'Ask her.'

I told him I would. Then he'd look like an idiot. Then he'd be embarrassed. As I went to pick up the phone, he confessed: he hadn't kissed her after all. But he had taken the mushrooms, and he grabbed my arm in a final attempt to convince me.

Sitting out in Juliette's courtyard, the last piece of reheated pizza cold between us, and me now feeling well and truly drunk on my fourth beer, I asked how Camille was.

'Married money,' Juliette told me.

'Eddie was in love with her.'

'Everyone was in love with Camille. All my own boyfriends included.' Juliette grinned, picking at a fleck of tobacco caught near her chipped front tooth. 'So when did he do it?' she asked, and I knew she was referring to Eddie.

It was when he was seventeen. A couple of years after my father lost all his money and we moved away, to a flat on the other side of the overpass.

'But it wasn't that,' I said. 'When you're a kid you don't care about money, or your house, or any of that. It wasn't even the fights between my parents. He was just one of those people.' I could see her looking at me. 'He never fitted in, and because he wanted to be liked so badly, other kids were cruel.'

I remembered one of them taking Eddie's school shorts and leaving him, knees together, hands trying to cover himself as he walked home. And then there was the time he was bashed, nose broken and bloody, weeping as my mother asked him who had done this to him.

'Later on there were the drugs. We all took them. But they messed with him.'

It was easy now to provide a list of possible reasons, all I should have seen at the time, and probably did see, but I always felt that somehow, in the tangle of isolated incidents, I had never grasped the larger whole, the truth of what had taken him further than he should ever have gone.

Juliette put her cigarette out. 'You know he lost his virginity to me. One of those times I babysat you, and he came home later.'

'Well, that would have made him happy.' I smiled at Juliette, who was standing now, beer in one hand.

'Want to see my paintings?' She nodded in the direction of the sunroom at the back of the house.

I had noticed the canvases stacked against the wall when I came in, and I'd been curious, wanting to pull one out, unable to imagine how Juliette would paint. Something unfinished, I thought. I followed her now, into the narrow room, lit only by a single bulb hanging from the ceiling. She turned the first of the paintings around and stepped back so that she, too, could assess them.

It was difficult to see it properly, there on the ground, the light too dim to show the depths of soft darkness. There was a bridge spanning the night and a low cloud, barely visible, pressing down, heavy and sombre on the earth below.

'Can you hold it up?' I said.

Resting her drink on the window ledge, she obliged, head cocked to one side as she watched me, observing.

In the distance I could see a light, only small, illuminating one corner of the canvas a little more brightly than the other. I leant closer and, having drunk too much, almost knocked the painting out of her grasp. She steadied herself, never taking her eyes off me as she waited for my reaction.

'God, it's good,' I said.

She turned another around and then another, and I sat on the floor in the middle of her sunroom as she held them up for me one by one, each a world so dark you wanted to step right in to see if you could touch what you felt was there but was never quite discernible.

I was about eight when Susie's mother, Sarah, gave Eddie and me the IQ test. Sarah was studying psychology at university and she must have asked my mother if she could use us as her subjects. We went, not entirely sure what we were expected to do, just wanting a break in the monotony of a weekend that had entailed more bickering than usual.

We let ourselves in through the tall wooden gate. The Acott house was one of the largest in the neighbourhood, surrounded by an overgrown garden, the weeds knee high and sticky, the trees pressing against the windows. Inside the dark hall, it was quiet. Everyone seemed to be out. Eddie called hello, his voice unsteady. I shouted a little louder, and Sarah appeared, her footsteps soft as she came out of the lounge. She was a thin woman, her hair streaked with grey, her skin smeared with pale freckles. She was wearing glasses, which made the occasion much more serious than I had thought it was.

'Now, who first?' she said. 'Eddie or Lena?'

I was surprised she knew our names, because although I had been there to play a few times and her daughters had babysat us, she'd never seemed to register who we were. This was a house in which the adults had little presence. The children did as they pleased, helping themselves to the food they wanted, leaving the mess they made, fighting without intervention, turning on the television whenever they desired; it was chaotic and busy. But on that day it was quiet.

'Is Susie home?' I asked, once it had been determined that Eddie would go first and I would be left to wait.

Sarah wasn't sure where she was, and she looked at me for an instant, as if uncertain as to whether she should trouble herself with finding me an amusement. There was nothing at hand, and so she left me to sit on a sofa in the lounge.

With big windows that let in the northern light, it was the only sunny room in the house. The couch was warm, and I stretched out my legs on the cushions, surprised by all the cuts and scratches I had accumulated. Then, bored with this, I wandered around, picking up things and putting them back: a vase, a family photo in a frame, a bruised piece of fruit in a bowl on a table next to one of the armchairs. This was a grown-up room, one where there was little for me to do. I would have gone upstairs to the girls' bedrooms or out to the family room at the back of the house, but I wasn't sure when Sarah would be calling me.

I went to the kitchen instead and opened the fridge. Dinners had been left in casserole dishes, the food crusty now. Cheese was unwrapped and hard at the edge. There was a glass bowl with jelly, and I ran my finger through the middle, cutting a line that wobbled through the raspberry, hastily licking it off when I heard the door to the lounge open, followed by Sarah's voice saying my name.

'There you are.'

I looked around for Eddie, and she told me he'd headed home. 'I won't keep you long,' she promised.

The room off the lounge (which was, I suppose, a breakfast room) had bookshelves around two of the walls, dog-eared paperbacks stuffed into each shelf. The floor was covered with papers, stacked in piles that threatened to topple any second. Under the window, there was a round table, with four wooden shapes on top of it: a circle, a square, a triangle and a hexagon.

We were going to play a game, Sarah explained as she pulled out a seat for me. 'It's called Find the Smartie. I want you to close your eyes when I tell you and then pick the shape that has the Smartie underneath it.'

It seemed both easy and pointless.

'You can eat any Smarties you find,' Sarah said. 'Or save them to take them home.'

I shrugged. 'Sure.'

The game must have lasted about fifteen minutes,

maybe less. I closed my eyes when I was instructed. Sometimes Sarah asked me questions while I waited for her to choose her hiding place, strange questions that I attempted to answer. When I was allowed to look, I picked shapes randomly, with mixed success. The few Smarties I won, I ate immediately. I was thirsty and didn't want them, but didn't know how I was going to carry them on my bike.

At home, Eddie's Smarties were in a bowl. I didn't know how he'd got so many.

'I won them.' He spoke with an icy triumph that was unfamiliar. 'It was an IQ test.'

I had no idea what he was talking about.

'A test to see how smart we are. How quickly we figure out the pattern and find the Smarties.'

'No it wasn't.'

Eddie began to count his out — slowly, carefully.

'You're lying.'

He ate one, eyeing me as he did so.

'It was just a game.'

'Was it?'

His smirk made me want to punch him.

'She never said it was a test.'

'Yes, she did.' He ate another Smartie. 'Besides, it was obvious. To those of us with high IQs.'

'What a load of crap.' I tried to hit him but only succeeded in sending all the Smarties scattering to the floor.

Eddie seized me in a headlock and I kicked him. We rolled onto the ground, crushing the Smarties beneath our body weight. When I bit him, he screamed.

Later that day, I rode my bike along the back streets that led to Susie's house. It was almost evening and the lights were on in the upstairs windows. The front door was open, and I could hear the TV from inside and music coming from one of the bedrooms. I had crept out of our house and ridden over there because I had thought I wanted to talk to Sarah. I hadn't envisaged encountering the rest of the family, and now that this seemed possible, I was less certain of my mission.

I stood at the front door, and then, feeling foolish and embarrassed, decided to go home. As I picked up my bike, Sarah peered out.

'It wasn't fair,' I told her, when she realised it was only me standing there, hesitant, eyes still red from crying after being punished for the fight with Eddie.

We sat together on the sandstone paving that surrounded the house, our backs against the wall as she tried to understand.

'What were our marks?' I wiped at my nose, smearing grease from my bike across my cheek.

They were both high, she said.

Was Eddie a genius?

According to the test, he was certainly in the upper levels.

And me? Was I a genius, too?

She blinked nervously as she tried to explain that the test was just one measure of intelligence.

It was wrong, I said.

She waited for me to continue. At only eight years old, it wasn't easy to explain why I felt there had been an injustice.

The garden was in darkness now; only the camellia bushes that grew near the house were visible. At my feet a few bruised heads had fallen onto the sandstone, the petals crushed underfoot, their thick perfume sweet against the smell of mud, dirt and leaves. I picked one up and pulled it apart, the bloom silky to the touch.

She would take me home. My mother would be worried. And she stood slowly, reaching down for me. I didn't take her hand. Lifting my bike up again, I told her I would be fine. 'It's just around the corner.'

It was too dark. She would get her keys and we could put the bike in the boot. 'I won't be a second,' she said.

But I didn't wait. Swinging my leg over the crossbar, I rode down the garden path and out onto the street, the coolness of the night soothing as I pedalled faster, the wind in my hair and the rush of air against my skin as I turned down the steep hill that led to the river.

At home, they didn't hear me. My parents sat in the kitchen, discussing Eddie's test results, while in the sunroom, Eddie watched television, holding frozen peas to the black eye I had given him.

'I worry about Lena,' my mother told my father. 'She is so angry.'

'You worry about Lena?' He was surprised.

I stayed perfectly quiet.

'Maybe she is jealous of him?'

I could tell my mother didn't believe her own words.

'Maybe we don't give her enough attention?'

With my ear pressed against the door, I clenched my fingers in the palm of my hand, white-knuckled and silent. They had got it so wrong. But I stayed where I was, listening to them searching, fumbling for an answer, while I remained unable to explain what it was that had upset me.

As I sat on my bed, having left Juliette still drinking beer in her sunroom, I could articulate, with a concise clarity that had eluded me back then, why I felt there had been an injustice.

You see, I would say if I could inhabit my eight-year-old self, I thought it was just a matter of random chance. I should have been told that there was a predetermined pattern for me to decipher, and rules to follow.

But at the time, when it had mattered so much, I had been unable to find words for all I felt.

I got into bed. Somewhere, in a suburb nearby, Jono would be lying next to his new girlfriend, one arm half draped across her body. Up and down my street, people slept in pairs, children dreamt, and dogs and cats curled up in baskets. And then there were the others, houses with people like us. At the time, I had backed away from Juliette's casual grouping of the two of us. But perhaps she was right. Like her, I was alone. Sometimes I thought of it as freedom, but I had come to be less sure now that I was here in an empty house I called home, a place where the wind was liable to rush through the gaps under the doors, as sudden and cold as the fear of having once again missed what matters.

Just a Wedding

On her first morning in Madrid, Emma woke with the sun piercing through the gap in a shutter, a single bright slice across the room. She'd been dreaming of wedding cakes, elaborate creations covered in thick marzipan and decorated with birds, twisted vines, clusters of flowers and twirls of leaves. The chef who brought them to her presented each one proudly, placing it on the table and waiting for her approval.

'It's beautiful,' she would tell him, and it always was — at first glance. But if she examined the cake more closely, she would see the flaws in its smooth surface: a tracing of cracks, a dove with a broken beak, petals that had been carelessly crushed. No, it wasn't good enough, she was sorry, he would need to try again; and his disappointment was evident as he picked up the plate and took it away.

She shook off the dream, hating its cheap obviousness,

and sat up slowly. Next to her, Charles was still asleep, his eyelids waxy, his mouth slightly open, his breath stale. She could smell sangria, like rotten fruit, overripe in the room. His dark curls were damp across his forehead; a fly buzzed, and then settled on his shoulder. She shifted away from him carefully, not wanting to wake him, because then she could no longer be alone. The tiled floor was cold, and she waited for her eyes to fully adjust as she took in the dimmer recesses, trying to remember which door led to the cubicle with the washbasin and toilet.

They had been married a fortnight ago. It was Charles who'd suggested it, drunk and exuberant when she'd got her PhD, and a job in the medical research department at the university. He'd pulled her close in the restaurant, kissing her deeply, and then he'd proposed. Well, he hadn't proposed as such, he'd said: 'Let's have a wedding.' And when she'd laughed, he'd told her it would be fun. 'We can have a party, get presents, go on a honeymoon, just like they do in the movies. The Continent, just the two of us. We'll stay in hotels, have sex all day and all night, maybe go out and get drunk for a couple of hours and then come back and have sex again.'

They'd only known each other for a month, she'd protested.

'But that's when you should get married. You don't want to wait until you know each other. Who'd get married then? You have to do it while you still find each other irresistible.'

There was something thrilling to it: the well-trodden road towards marriage far below them both, dusty, dry and ignored.

'Besides, if it doesn't work, we can always undo it.' He raised his glass.

'I don't think that's the point of a wedding.' She'd laughed a little nervously.

'Why does it have to have a point? Why can't it just be what it is? A wedding. A moment.' He topped up both their drinks. 'To us. And our impending nuptials.'

They had married that weekend.

They hadn't had a party — in fact, they hadn't told anyone. They'd gone to the registry on a bus, both dressed in jeans and T-shirts, and she'd felt like a child on a dare that she no longer wanted to participate in.

Nor were there any presents, although her parents had given them money to travel. Not that this was a wedding gift: it was a present to her, her father had insisted, as congratulations for the PhD and the job, so she could have a holiday before she started work.

'You could have just lived together,' he told her, and she felt ashamed of the foolishness of it all.

'I know.'

But she never would have just lived with Charles. If he'd asked her to move in, rather than marry him, she would have said no. She didn't want to live with him now. This wasn't about her feelings for him, it was more about her own strange inclination to try on the clothes of another woman, someone more colourful than she had ever been. And yet, as she took the cheque from her father, she felt like a silly child again, this time in an outfit that was too large, and — quite frankly — embarrassing in its glary flamboyance.

'It was just a wedding,' she said.

He took her hand. He was a gentle man who had always loved her with a calm kindness. 'Perhaps I'm old,' he said. 'And foolish or superstitious. It disturbs me to simply flout tradition, with no reason or thought.'

And although she didn't admit it, Emma knew exactly what he meant.

They'd spent her parents' money on two economy airfares — London, Lisbon, Madrid — and booked cheap rooms in hotels with websites that promised far more than they were ever going to deliver. At first the thrill of travel had been enough to keep her buoyant in pretending she was happy, but soon his constant presence had begun to close in on her, day and night, night and day. Just the two of them. A married couple. On a honeymoon. Even he had begun to stop uttering any of those phrases as she shrank away from words that had quickly become too large in their emptiness.

Now, in their Madrid hotel room, she switched her phone on to see the time. She'd been asleep for just a couple of hours. She drank a glass of water greedily. She was parched, like the sunken hide of a cow dead in a ravine, she thought, skin like leather, collapsed on bleached white bones, and she glanced quickly in the bathroom mirror, relieved to see that this spectre of death didn't return her gaze. It was just herself, blotched and red-eyed from too much drink. Nothing more, nothing less.

In the bed, Charles shifted in his sleep.

She studied him, his fleshy bottom lip, the line of his jaw, the stubble that peppered his cheeks and the fine crust of sleep in his eyelashes. She turned away, and then back again, surprised at the wave of repulsion she felt when she contemplated how familiar and yet unfamiliar he was to her.

The previous night, they had drunk too much, wandering the streets and stopping to have another (often two or three for him, thrown back with increasing speed as he talked — ludicrous flights of fancy — while she sat in silence) and then another.

In the third bar, they found themselves wedged in a corner with Jose and Lois, two Puerto Ricans from New York who were doing Europe in a week. A country a day, and they counted those they had done and those they were yet to do, leaving Emma wondering how you 'did' a country.

Charles had insisted that they all call him Carlos.

'This is who I am now.' He stood on his bar stool, pointing at his chest. 'Carlos.'

'You're no Carlos,' Jose had told him. 'You're as white as …' He'd grinned as he'd tried to summon up a suitable comparison, until his gaze settled back on Emma. 'As white as she is, man. As white as she is.'

Charles grinned back. 'Ah, but I'm Mediterranean on the inside.'

Lois wanted champagne, not wine, and she shouted across the bar, her Spanish fluent, her accent causing considerable confusion. The barman turned to Emma as he poured Lois's drink, his wink slow and deliberate. She looked down at the counter in embarrassment.

'Pity you're married.' Lois fished an olive out of the bowl in front of her, bright red fingernails flashing against her lips. 'Cos he's got eyes for you, honey.'

'But I'm not married,' Emma said. 'I'm just pretending.'

Lois flung her head back and laughed, throatily. She tapped her fingernails on the coaster, the sharp rap in time to the music. 'Jose,' and she called his name insistently, 'let's dance, baby. Let's get outta here and dance.'

He ignored her.

She stood, towering in heels that provided so little balance, yet she managed to defy this, swaying over to Jose, who continued to ignore her. She turned to Charles. 'Carlos, baby, I wanna dance.'

Charles's bow was low and sweeping. He took Lois by the arm, nodding at Jose. 'She wants to dance.'

But Jose's hand was raised in the air, his voice ringing out above the din of the bar, ordering another drink, another jug of wine for his friends over there and he pointed to a group of students in the corner.

'Charles can take you dancing,' Emma said. 'We'll find you.'

'And leave you?' Charles seized her, drawing her close and kissing her on the lips. 'Carlos does not leave his woman.'

Later, as they walked home through the chill streets of Madrid, the four of them weaving from pavement to pavement, Charles and Jose had started singing, strange made-up harmonies that drifted through the night air.

'You sing like' — Jose kissed the tips of his fingers, gesturing towards the black sky — '*angelitos negros.*'

And they had made promises of breakfast, coffee and churros, the names of places thrown around, until Señora from the hotel had opened the door and shouted at them, and Emma had apologised, rushing towards the entrance before it was closed in their face.

Now, as Emma stood in the wash cubicle and rinsed herself, she saw her bag on the floor, passport and wallet tucked into an inside pocket, clothes for today neatly folded on top of her suitcase.

She brushed her teeth, taking care to be quiet, and dressed in the dim light. The door was heavy, and she kept hold of it as she let it swing shut behind her. Sitting on the tiles of the top step, she put her shoes on, her fingers shaking slightly as she tied the laces. Perhaps it was the cold, or her hangover, she told herself, not wanting to admit that this tremor may have been due to a fear of what she could do. Standing quickly, and without glancing back, she headed down the stairs towards the street.

Emma had never been in love. She had gone out with men, the relationship always dwindling away after a few months, the calls and dates becoming less frequent, the need to define the ending assiduously avoided on her part, but if she had to be dragged into such a talk, she was always reasonable.

She enjoyed her own company, and she liked her work. She could spend hours shaping and framing a clinical trial, lost in defining the questions, establishing the parameters, laying the paths that would lead to a conclusion.

As she stood at the entrance to the hotel, she wondered why she had turned so far from herself. Perhaps it was having finished studying, or maybe she had simply been lifted off the ground by the enthusiasm with which Charles had taken her hand, leading her in a direction she should have only glanced towards.

He was an AV tech at the university. She had walked into the lecture theatre to find him singing to himself, the timbre of his voice caught by the microphone, the slow rise of the song filling the room. He had been setting up the theatre for a presentation by the newly appointed professor in her department.

He was completely unembarrassed when he saw her, and asked how she would like to be miked, from the stand or on a lapel?

'It's not me who's talking,' she explained. 'I'm just checking that the video conference is working.'

'All in order.' He switched the display between screenshots of the different campuses and showed her which controls to use. 'Call me if you forget — or if anything goes wrong.'

She'd seen him later that day in the canteen. He'd brought his lunch over to where she sat reading, and they talked, his voice lilting, his hands darting around as he told her about his family, his love of music and painting and writing, his sister who had died of an overdose, the first time he'd had his heart broken, his brief stint as a yoga teacher followed by a job as the personal assistant to a minor celebrity on the dive, his tales slapping up against each other like a choppy sea dancing under the light.

She'd loved the ease with which he'd entertained her, the colour of his stories, the wiry restlessness of his entire being as he talked, the possibility of a life that could constantly change direction.

Emma, on the other hand, was the only child of two doctors; she had studied hard at school, gone to university and continued with research, never once thinking there could be any approach other than a careful progress towards some kind of ultimate goal. She ate well to be healthy, she exercised four times a week to stay slim, she worked hard to further her academic career. Charles had been so foreign, she remembered. It was like being given an exotic animal, a species so rare and different that she had wanted to observe it closely. And yet at any other time she might only have taken a cursory glance, putting it back on the table immediately.

She thought of him now, up in that room, the shutters closed to the morning.

On their third night together, he had told her he had never left anyone. 'I have always been left.'

She had ignored the alarm she felt, watching him lying next to her, staring at the ceiling as he spoke.

'Well, maybe with me it will be different,' she'd said, surprised at how fervently she hoped that it would be the case.

He had laughed, asking her what she planned to do to make him run, and she had made up scenarios in which she behaved abominably, forcing him away, disturbed by the relish she felt at these imagined renditions of herself.

Not far off she could hear shouts, whistles, the sound of a crowd, and she stepped back into the doorway as the noise grew in intensity. It was a demonstration, all women, waving placards, with one word over and over again: *domicilio*. Something to do with the home, she presumed. She had no idea. She just had to wait as they made their way down Calle Mayor, a rush of sound and feet, voices in unison. And then, as quickly as they had descended, the women were gone, leaving her on the edge of the street, ready to walk.

The air was sharp and clear with the last of the winter

snows high on the mountains, as she followed streets she did not know. A group of children ran to the train; clustered close, they laughed and jostled each other, their uniforms clean, white shirts startling against olive skin, navy gabardine pressed in perfect pleats. And on each of the street corners, the blind waited with their canes, trays around their necks, selling *lotería* tickets.

Emma kept walking. At the Buen Retiro Park — or at least this was what she assumed it must be, having read about it in a guidebook — she stood at the entrance, the first of the spring leaves floating in the morning light, and the lake glittering slate smooth in the distance.

Old men played boules, women walked children in strollers, and there was a café where waiters in stiff white coats served coffee and iced lemon drinks. Despite her thirst, she went on, until finally, under the arches of the Rosaleda, she stopped.

In front of her was a statue. She would not have even noticed it if the women next to her had not been looking at it. Both middle-aged, both speaking with American accents, they stood, one with a guidebook, the other with a camera. It was a monument to Lucifer falling from heaven, the only known public statue of the devil, the woman with the guidebook explained, taking her glasses off.

Emma was surprised. He was just like any angel, powerful wings straining up against the sky. A serpent was pulling him back to earth. She stayed where she was, staring at it, tired now. She had walked for far longer than she had thought she would, the fear of what she was capable of fizzing through her blood, speedy with the sugar of adrenaline.

Closing her eyes to the morning light, she imagined finding her way along the myriad roads and streets and laneways she had wandered, returning to the stairs that led up to the room where the man who was her husband was probably still asleep. She winced.

In the hotel room there was a suitcase of clothes, and she went through them in her mind — jeans, T-shirts, swimmers, sandals, a favourite cardigan.

In her handbag she had money and her passport. She ran her fingers over the leather, feeling the shape of her wallet and papers. Her picture was the same on her driver's licence as her passport, wide blue eyes staring straight at the camera, dark hair cropped short. The photo was taken a year ago, showing her as she was before she met Charles.

'You look so serious,' he had said.

'I am serious,' she had replied, taking the passport back from him.

'I am, too,' he had said and she had laughed at him.

'But I am,' he had protested. 'Not in the same way you are. But no less.'

He was serious. She knew this now. His love for her was serious; his desire to marry her, flippant as it had seemed, weighed far more than her feeble attempt to pretend it didn't matter. And she wanted nothing more than to abandon him — the cruelty of it far worse than anything she had ever done. To run from this mistake and pretend that it never happened. To get a taxi to the airport and book the next flight home, where she would let herself into her old apartment, still hers in anticipation of a moment that she had always known would come.

Next to her, the woman with the guidebook was quick to dismiss the statue. 'I thought the devil would be far more interesting,' she said to her friend. 'But you wouldn't even know it was him.' She closed the book.

Emma didn't hear what she said next.

She was seeing herself as she once was, there at her front door, the bay window at the end of the hall, and the jacaranda outside. The longing for home and her previous life brought it all into sharp focus: her desk where she had studied for years; her bookshelf, ordered with journals and texts and the dozen or so novels she had indulged in without ever quite understanding what point there was to reading them. And if she turned to her right, she could walk through to the kitchen, clean, bare, functional, ready for her to cook the few meals she knew, and beyond that was her bedroom, hers.

She opened her eyes, to a world hovering on the edge of what she could do.

'Shall we go?' the woman with the guidebook asked her friend, already turning to head out of the Rosaleda.

Emma watched her, trim in khaki pants, a white

T-shirt and flat leather sandals, her bag slung across her shoulder, unaware that her friend had failed to follow her.

The other woman had remained. Taking a few steps forward, she put out her hand, walking like the blind, towards a statue that held her attention. Emma understood it: that desire to touch, despite knowing just how the stone would feel, cold and smooth beneath the skin if you could, in fact, run your hands over it. But you couldn't. To do so would mean crossing the carefully planted garden that surrounded the fountain, and then stepping into the water itself, only to discover that the devil was too high to reach. It was just a brief desire, and the logistics of carrying it out were far too troublesome. The woman let her hand drop, and then she saw Emma, watching her, and she hurried after her friend, embarrassed.

Alone now, Emma remained still in the face of her urge to run.

It was just a wedding, she'd told her father, hating how false her words were. It could be undone, Charles had said, his flippancy about the event also a lie. And staring up at the statue, Emma bit her lip as she imagined herself fleeing without a word, the temptation so strong. But she wasn't the woman they'd both pretended she was. She let her fingers slide off her wallet and passport, the adrenaline gone now, and she tried to remember the path she had taken so she could return to say goodbye.

The Bad Dog Park

Each morning Pete woke, ready to feed Doris by seven a.m. He gave her a cup of dry biscuits and one hundred grams of mince, pre-measured and kept in plastic bags at the bottom of the fridge. There were times when he had to coax her to eat, and other times when she barked too eagerly, leaping up to lick scraps he left on the table, her hunger an indication that her blood sugar levels were wrong.

While she ate, he washed his face, splashing cold water on his skin to wake up, so that he could measure the dosage with a steady hand. The insulin needed to be gently rolled in his palms first, the cloudiness spreading evenly throughout the bottle. He liked to let it get a little warmer as well, to take the chill from the fridge out of the dosage. And then he had to slowly draw up the syringe, his worsening eyesight sometimes making exact measurements more challenging: fourteen intravenous units, no bubbles, no air pockets.

Over the last two years, Doris had never taken a needle easily. And nor had he.

When Sophia was a child, Kate took her for her shots. He had tried the first time, only to feel the horrifying lightness of panic flood through him, settling in his throat. The doctor had sent him out of the room, leaving Sophia screaming for him, terrified of being abandoned.

And then when Kate had been ill, there had been endless needles, her blood becoming such a familiar sight to him that he began to forget her surface: her bright eyes, pale skin and curly hair replaced by blood and vomit and shit and all the mechanics, the workings, like a toy pulled apart in a bad dream.

At seven-thirty he checked Doris had eaten all her food, and then he sat at the kitchen table and called her over, the syringe resting next to him. To his surprise she always came, eager-eyed, forgetting that the delivery of a liver treat invariably preceded the fright of an injection. Talking to her quietly, he fed her, stroking the wiry kinks in her fur, more in an effort to calm himself than her, her deep brown eyes fixed on him.

Sophia had brought Doris home five years ago. Thin, bedraggled and tucked in the folds of her coat, Doris had whimpered loud enough for him to hear her before he saw her. Unable to hide her any longer, Sophia had held her out in her shaking hands, talking too much as she usually did on the rare occasions she visited. 'See,' she said. 'She's sooo cute. Her little paws,' and Sophia stretched them towards him. 'Shake hands, Pete. There's a good girl, such a good girl, such a cute, good, little girl.' She burrowed her face in the puppy's tiny body, squeezing her too hard, the dog yelping and nipping in fright. 'Jesus. You fucking little bitch.'

The puppy pissed on the floor as soon as Sophia put her down.

'There's a rag under the sink,' Pete told her wearily.

Sophia ignored him. Standing at the back door, she lit a cigarette, inhaling deeply as she began to pace the courtyard. 'Have you got any money, Dad?'

He didn't answer her straightaway.

'I've been kicked out of my flat, and they won't give me back the bond. They're saying there's a rubbish removal and cleaning fee, a thousand bucks, and I'm broke, Dad. I'm so fucking broke.'

As he bent down to clean up the piss, the puppy lay on her back, paws in the air, fur thick beneath his fingers.

'What's she called?' he asked.

He scratched her under the chin, her hind leg thumping against the floor in a reflex reaction.

Sophia shrugged. 'How would I know?'

'I thought she was yours,' he said.

Her eyes were conniving; he didn't want to see it, but there it was, right in front of him, naked and sharp and ugly. 'I bought her for you, Dad. As a present. To thank you for always being so good to me. You're all I've got, you know.' She dropped her cigarette to the ground, stepping inside to hug him. 'So you name her. She's yours.' And she bent down to the puppy. 'She's sooo cute.'

He didn't want a dog. He told Sophia this.

'Well, I can't look after her.'

There was silence between them.

And then Sophia remembered why she had come. 'I've got nowhere to live, no money. How am I meant to even feed her?' She scooped the puppy up in her arms.

He sighed and opened his wallet.

But when she left, very soon afterwards, the puppy remained behind.

In the first year and a half, he would wake bleary-eyed to walk Doris around the parklands, trying to stop her from pulling him on the lead or, if he let her off, trying to get her to return. Crouched down, he would call her, coaxingly, lovingly, holding out treats for her, sometimes even weeping in frustration as she would stand perfectly still, watching him, poised to bolt the instant he attempted to seize her collar.

On one particular morning, he had tried for over an hour. He was late for work, a lecture to two hundred first-years on the role of media in government, and he knew that when he did make it in, there would be snickering, whispers about how hopeless he was. There were always lecturers who students thought were bumbling, useless, and only good for a high mark — and he was one of them.

'Could you grab her by the collar?' he called out to a woman who was walking five dogs of various sizes on a tangle of leads.

She seized Doris, keeping her apart from the other dogs with swift nudges. 'You'd better be quick,' she said. 'Six may well be the straw to break this camel's back.'

He snapped the lead on Doris and thanked her.

'Pity I don't have enough free hands to write down my number. Dog walking,' she added when she saw the confusion on his face. She grinned broadly. 'I'm not offering anything else.'

He apologised, embarrassed.

'She'd be one of the ones I take to the Bad Dog Park.'

'Is there a place with that name?' He realised how idiotic he sounded as soon as he asked the question.

'It's what I call it. The place where you take the ones who aren't so well behaved,' she said. 'The ones who drink, smoke, lie, cheat and steal.' She nodded in the direction of the station crossing. 'Over the railway bridge and behind the velodrome. It's one of the only untouched areas of park. Overgrown. No bike tracks or sporting fields.' She turned to keep walking. 'I'm there for the late-afternoon shift. Three p.m. onwards.'

He had passed there every day on the train, never thinking to walk Doris beyond this side of the tracks. The grass was uncut, growing in unruly clumps, insects whirring in the humidity of the afternoon, wild fennel in bunches of licorice sweetness, and overhead the white cockatoos screeched with a note of panic as they lurched and swooped and wheeled against the charcoal clouds.

She wasn't there. Admittedly, it had taken him three months to finally venture into the badlands, and he was a fool for thinking there would be some magical meeting, but he had hoped.

He let Doris off the lead, and she sniffed the breeze nervously.

'Go,' he told her, shooing her away with his hand.

Far off, by the velodrome carpark, he could see another dog — large, alsatian-like, the owner some distance away. Doris spotted it as well, and tail high, back straight, she loped towards it with an erect gait that was half bravado, half fear.

He had never witnessed a truly ferocious dogfight before. As he ran across the parkland, sweating and afraid, he could hear the snarling, and the yelps from Doris; he could see the owner kicking at them both, trying to separate them while keeping himself out of the fracas, his shouts panicked, the thud of his boot against the flank of the alsatian and then his own scream as he, too, was bitten.

Later, Pete had only a vague recollection of how they had managed to break up the fight. He remembered shouting at the man, telling him to control his dog and reaching for a stick, which he flailed uselessly, until one of them (it must have been the other man because he couldn't imagine it being himself) had dragged the alsatian out by its hind legs.

Doris had puncture wounds to be patched and antibiotics to take, and in the midst of this the vet had also taken a blood sample, as part of a free service offered during October. 'To check your dog's overall health.'

He didn't listen. He was too busy trying to soothe her.

Two days later, they called to tell him Doris was a diabetic.

'It's unusual,' the vet said, 'in a dog so young. But it happens.' Had she been drinking more, eating more? Was she urinating more frequently?

Pete hadn't noticed anything. But now he thought about it, it should have been obvious. She'd been scavenging in bins whenever he walked her, and twice in the last week she'd pissed inside.

To inject Doris, he had to pull up a scruff of skin on her neck.

'Make a tent,' the vet nurse instructed him, irritated that she had to demonstrate the technique again. 'And then you put the needle in. Here, you have a go.' She shoved a syringe into his hands.

He wanted to faint.

'It's just a needle,' she said. 'You'll get used to it.'

But he never did. Holding the loose skin in his hands, he felt sick at the thought of puncturing flesh, piercing through the warmth of her body. And Doris howled, head back (until he learnt to keep her steady), mouth open in abject terror; she howled and howled in deep shock. How could he do this to her? And yet he did. Every morning, and then again, every night.

'Oh for god's sake, just put her down,' Sophia told him.

It was a sentiment echoed by most.

Gretchen, who taught with him, listened in bemusement. 'It's ridiculous,' she scolded, as she frequently did. 'That much money on caring for a pet. There are people in Third World countries desperate for insulin, and here you are, giving it to an animal.'

He didn't know if she was correct about insulin need in other parts of the world, and he refrained from commenting on her newly purchased shoes (she'd just shown them to him and told him how much they cost). How many of the unshod across the globe could have had something on their feet for the price she'd paid?

The truth was he wanted to put Doris down every single morning and every single evening, but when he removed the syringe and began to breathe again, rubbing her neck and feeding her another treat, he told himself he would learn to cope. He was getting better at it. Surely that had been a little easier than the injection twelve hours ago? And why should his discomfort with needles cause the death of a living creature he had come to love?

At the end of summer he returned to the Bad Dog Park. Walking over the railway bridge and down the gravel path under the lemon-scented gums, he was a little wary.

There was no one in sight.

The ground was muddy beneath his feet, and the damp soaked through his shoes as he followed the track round to the open expanse, holding Doris on the lead until he could be sure all was safe. When he turned the corner, ready to let her go, he saw to his distress that there was a pack of dogs, five or six of them — all bad, no doubt; killers, probably — and he was tempted to slink away.

But then he noticed her.

Sitting in the grass, headphones in, oblivious to his approach until he was right behind her, she jumped, startled. He apologised for frightening her.

She didn't remember him, not at first, and when she did acknowledge some recollection of their meeting all that time ago, he wondered whether she was just making it up.

'You going to let her off?' she asked, nodding in Doris's direction. 'They're all okay.' She gestured at the pack, two of whom had begun circling Doris, sniffing her.

'I thought you said this was the Bad Dog Park.' He hesitated before undoing Doris's lead.

'Oh, they're bad,' she agreed. 'But not nasty bad. Just trouble in other ways.'

She asked him if he had ever walked along the tracks and up to the creek reserve.

He hadn't.

'Want to come?' She was standing now. 'My van's parked there. I need to load them up and deliver them back.'

Separated from the railway by cyclone fencing choked with lantana, purple heart and blackberries, the track they followed was little more than flattened grass, worn down by her daily trek there and back.

She told him she'd been walking dogs for ten years. 'I thought it was just going to be temporary, and then I couldn't see a reason to give it up.'

Didn't she get bored spending so much time on her own?

She contemplated his question with more seriousness than light conversation would ordinarily receive.

'Sometimes,' she eventually answered. 'There are days when I don't speak to a single person. I just sit in a park with dogs, and I wonder how they see me, and I think I could go crazy.'

He flicked a trail of bramble weed away with a stick. He knew what she meant. 'Some days I spend hours talking to hundreds and hundreds of students and I wonder the same thing.'

'When I was young, I thought I was going to be a doctor.' She bent down to pick up yet another piece of dog shit. 'There are some similarities between this' — she held up the bag — 'and the work of healthcare professionals.'

'I wanted to work in politics,' he told her. 'I quickly learnt that I was very unsuited.'

'But there are also days when I love this,' she said.

'At least you have that. I don't think I've felt that about my work for years. I know I should make some kind of change. I just seem to be very bad at that side of things.' He smiled at her. 'Hopeless at change, but very, very good at staying true and loyal and fulfilling my duty.' He stared up at the sky. 'And I'm not saying I'm a saint,' he rushed to add. 'My heart is bad. Desperate to do the wrong thing, and to hang out with the bad dogs.'

She grinned. 'Well, you're with 'em now.'

He flicked a fly away. 'Not really. I'm just tagging along.'

The first night he stayed at Marnie's house, he told her he would have to set the alarm early and leave.

'I'm sorry,' he said. 'It's the injection.'

They were lying next to each other, her hair like honey on his shoulder. He ran his hand gently down her body, resting on the line of her thigh. He knew he could be a little late administering the insulin, Doris would survive, but the truth was he needed his routine. This was the way he stayed calm. He wanted to explain this, but he felt so foolish.

She kissed him on the mouth. 'It's been five years since I've slept with anyone. I am very happy. You may feel free to leave whenever you need to.'

'But I'll be back,' he promised. 'Commitment is not my problem.'

He woke, well before the alarm of course, leaving her in bed and walking through the winter streets alone. Just him and the occasional shift worker, houses dark, curtains drawn.

He remembered his life with Kate, the time when, together with Sophia, they had been one of those dark houses, the three of them seemingly safe, nestled in a smooth knot of family, close and whole. For years his whole being had ached to return to that place. He could have sat, knees to chest, and rocked himself in grief and longing, a desire to go back, forever and ever. He had fought to close himself off from that, gasping for air and eventually able to stay above the surface by doing the right thing, by which he meant doing what he knew he should do, day after day, always aware of the depths beneath.

He opened his front door to find Doris, pressed against the other side, fast asleep at the end of the hallway. She lifted her head and thumped her tail, a thud on the floorboards, and she was up, eager to greet him.

Seven a.m. One hundred grams of mince, one cup of dog biscuits.

Splashing his face in the bathroom, he tried to remove all memory of the night before, the smell of Marnie lingering on his fingertips. He wanted to focus on the task at hand.

Ten past seven. Insulin out of fridge.

Rolling the bottle between his palms, he watched the

cloudiness spread through the liquid. He had a syringe ready and he uncapped it, taking care not to let his eyes linger on the steely point of the needle. With the bottle upside down, he pierced the rubber stopper and began to draw out an amount that far exceeded the dosage, carefully pushing the plunger back in until he reached a place that was close to fourteen units. He held it up to the light and searched for his glasses on the kitchen table, just to make sure.

Doris had not eaten all her food.

Calling her back outside, he tried to coax her towards the bowl. She started to cough, a hacking half bark, her back arching, and he was scared she was going to vomit, leaving nothing in her belly. He would have to call the emergency vet to check whether he should be skipping her dosage, and if he needed to bring her in. He looked at his watch. He was meant to be at work in two hours.

And then she stopped.

Head down in her bowl, she finished it all.

Seven-thirty. She sat at his feet, paws neatly in front of her, eyes resting on him while she waited for her treat, and accepted another as he ran his fingers through her coat and apologised for leaving her alone all night, talking nonsense until he felt calm enough to lift the scruff of her neck and plunge the needle in, to a howl that cut through the veil of serenity he had tried to cloak them both in, flimsy as always in the face of both their distress.

'Oh, Doris.' He put his head in his hands.

Her tail was thumping again, the horror forgotten as quickly as it had descended.

'Why do you do that?'

Of course she didn't answer.

Taking a deep breath, he re-capped the needle and put it in the sharps disposal container. Tonight would be better.

Marnie didn't mind him leaving her place so early.

'But you could just bring Doris here with you. Or we could stay at yours.' She kissed him on the eyelids, her mouth sweet in the darkness.

Pete tried to explain. 'There are some things I am good at. Like ignoring how little respect I receive from students. Like cooking a perfect roast chicken. Like giving every essay a distinction, no matter how bad it is. I'm also very good at cleaning a bathroom, and I can fix broken-down electrical equipment — DVD players that don't open, toasters with blown fuses.' He could sense her looking at him. 'But I am very bad with needles. And I mean truly terrible.'

He waited for her to suggest that he didn't have to do it. That he could put Doris down.

She remained silent.

'And I just need to be alone.' He didn't know how else to say it.

She was staring at the ceiling, eyes open, considering his words. He was coming to know the profile of her face, the shape of her gradually imprinting itself on his skin; his hands and mouth able to tell the story of her body now.

He could love her, he realised, and the sense was enough to make him reel, light-headed, until she shifted, just a little, and curved into him.

'Perhaps you could let me inject her for you.' She handed him the alarm clock as she spoke.

Two days later, they were walking along the tracks, the pack of dogs in front of them, the first warmth of spring in the evening air, when he asked her to come back to his place.

'I want to make you dinner,' he said. 'And be your host.'

She told him she would love that.

She didn't mention the needle, not then, not when he set his alarm, not when he crept out of bed at dawn, beckoning Doris to follow him down to the kitchen, trying to be quiet, even though he knew Marnie was probably lying awake in his room.

As he rolled the syringe in his palms, she came into the kitchen and held out her hand. 'Here, let me try.'

He explained the process, anxious that she understood every detail. She assured him she would be fine and she waved him away, telling him to go and have a shower.

The howl that morning was worse than ever. Marnie swore, the needle and insulin clattering to the floor.

Doris had bitten her, the teeth marks white on her skin.

Oh god, he was sorry. He was so sorry.

She rubbed at the wound in shock. 'No wonder you hate it so much.'

He still had to inject Doris. 'She's never done that with me,' he said. 'I mean, she howls like the devil in pain, but not that.'

Marnie checked her skin wasn't broken. 'For someone with a needle phobia, you've certainly had to deal with needles in the worst possible way.'

He had told her about Kate, and Sophia — who was currently off heroin but relying heavily on methadone. He had told her everything, and she, too, had told him about herself — the marriage to a man who had left her for her sister, the split within her family back in the States, her relationships since. They had given each other their past in words.

She sat opposite, her face still pale, her hair as kinked as Doris's coat, her breath slightly stale. He took her hand.

'Will it be easier for you if I'm not here?' she said.

He nodded. 'I think it's better if I do this alone. It might change. But just for now.'

She was silent, her fingers rolling the syringe around on the table, and then she realised what she was doing. Next to her, the box was full of them. 'God, there's a lot.'

'Two a day. Every day.'

Doris was lying at their feet. She lifted her head as

Marnie bent down, nervously, and stroked her.

'Well,' she said, 'I guess you could call that a bummer.'

And although her voice was light, he saw that there had been a shift, a moment of stepping back and looking at him and this predicament.

Six months later, Pete stands in his kitchen, watching Doris eat. He is breathing slowly, trying to still himself. He remembers therapists in the months after Kate had died telling him to be in the present, right now, step by step.

On the night of her death, she had been alone. He had sat by her bed all day, finally leaving her at eight to pick Sophia up from her friend's house.

They had thought she would make it to the morning, but she didn't. An hour after he left, he received the call at home.

'She was in peace,' the doctor promised him. 'She didn't even stir.'

He had held Sophia close, trying to find the words to tell her.

Friends had thought he was courageous, a wonderful father, extraordinary in his strength — 'admirable' was a word they frequently used. But he knew the truth. There had been months when he had barely spoken, fulfilling his duties — homework supervised, dinners and lunches made, excursion notes completed, house cleaned — with no notion of joy.

Doris nudges her bowl against the back wall. She has not left a scrap.

Over the last months, he has crept towards this day, moving like a man on a ledge. And now he is here, and it is not a moment he wants to be in.

He picks the dish up and washes it under the tap, but doesn't know where to put it. There is so much stuff, he realises — her biscuit tin, her bed, the bag that he takes with him when he walks her, her tennis ball, her lead, her water bowl — and then there is all the paraphernalia for her diabetes.

'Unfortunately, there is a needle involved,' the vet explained to him when he called yesterday to make the appointment. 'But we can sedate her first.'

And me? he wanted to ask. Could you also sedate me?

Doris is sitting by his side, waiting for her treat.

He smooths back the hair that grows in tufts, like bushy brows, above her eyes, talking to her as he always does, soothing with his words.

Sophia promised she would be here by nine.

There are still five minutes to go.

Fifteen minutes later, he realises he is going to have to do this alone.

He snaps the lead on Doris and takes her out to the car, still not sure if he will change his mind.

'It's okay,' Marnie had told him each morning he had left her at her house, walking back through the empty streets to his own home. Sometimes he had tried to read her, to see whether it actually was still okay, but he had never been able.

And then he saw it: the shift he had noticed that first morning in his kitchen had inched a little further, an almost imperceptible movement, an awareness that this was dividing them.

She was offered a friend's apartment in New York for a month. She needed to see friends she had lost touch with, perhaps try to reconnect with family; she would so love it if he could be with her.

And he said no.

It was the cost, he tried to explain. Eighty dollars a day for a vet nurse to care for Doris and administer her insulin. It was just impossible.

'Of course,' she said.

That night she didn't ask him to stay. 'I need to sleep,' she explained. 'When you leave at dawn, I wake.'

He said he understood. He suggested she stay at his house again. He assured her it would be fine, but the first time, he lost his nerve and failed to get the whole dose into Doris, and the second time, he dropped the bottle of insulin.

He can do this.

Doris leaps into the back, delighted at the prospect of a ride in the car with him. He has the keys in his hand, cold in his grasp. He cannot think about the act of walking her into the surgery, holding the lead in his hands, reassuring her it will be alright as she suddenly

GEORGIA BLAIN

realises where he has taken her and refuses to take those last steps, through the swinging doors, with him.

He has not told Marnie of his decision. Will she look at him with horror? Is he someone who can kill a dog just so he can go away with her? He does not know what he will tell her, or how. Perhaps he could say that Doris was hit by a car. He imagines attempting to lie, and he knows he will stutter and stumble, eventually confessing.

He cannot do this.

Opening his door, he puts one leg down on the road, the tar hot beneath the soles of his shoes.

This is not who he is.

His phone rings. It is Sophia.

'Oh god, Dad.' Her voice is slurred, sleepy, and he knows she is not even out of bed. 'I'm sorry. But you'll be okay.'

He tells her it's fine.

'So, you've done it?' she asks.

He opens the back window, giving Doris some air, stroking her as he does so. He has to make a decision. Get her inside and give her the insulin, or start the car.

'I don't know what to do,' he says, and he stares up at the blank blue sky.

Sophia is silent on the other end. She has probably nodded off.

'I'm sorry,' he says softly. He puts the phone down on the seat next to him, and he doesn't know who he is apologising to: Kate, Sophia, Marnie, Doris? He has tried so hard to do the right thing and he has failed each of them.

Doris is waiting patiently for their journey to begin, but his courage is leaving him. Soon he will get out of the car, and she will jump down after him. They will head back into the house, where he will inject her as he should have done hours ago, and he will work on an article he is writing, and later in the afternoon, he will take her to meet Marnie at the Bad Dog Park, where they will talk, both knowing that this hairline crack is widening, separating them as it grows, until they are no longer able to bridge a distance that he wants to close before it is too late.

And so he shuts the car door, and buckles his seatbelt, hoping he can finally turn his back on the dutiful man that holds him too close. That man has served his purpose. What's required now is a different kind of man, a man that can walk into the vet with his dog and say *I've had enough, I want to put this dog down* — he just doesn't know if he can get there alone.

'Marnie,' he says when she answers. She waits for him to continue. 'I'm sitting in my car with Doris.'

She is silent at first. 'Okay.'

He breathes a little more. 'Can you come over?'

When she finally speaks, her voice is quiet. 'I'm picking up the morning shift.'

She is walking the small dogs, the ones who behave. She takes them around the paths on this side of the tracks, delivering them home before she collects the bad ones for the afternoon. 'Can you wait an hour?'

He could delay the appointment until she can go with him. But he knows that if he puts it off now, he won't get there at all and, besides, she shouldn't have to be part of this. 'It's okay,' he tells her, doing his best to sound convincing. He is about to hang up, when she asks him to wait.

'I'll be there soon.'

He sits on the back seat with Doris, her warm breath in his ear, until there are only ten minutes left before he is due at the vet's.

He has to do this.

He cannot wait any longer.

He sends Marnie a text, telling her he will be okay. As he pulls out onto the road, he sees her in the rear-vision mirror, but he doesn't stop. He has needed to get to this place for years, and he has to keep going because this frail breath of change that is so very terrifying must be fanned, enough to give him the strength to do what he should be doing. 'I'm sorry,' he says again, but this time he knows who he is talking to. He can see him, the man he once was, right there in the rear-vision mirror, and he is sorry to go against all that has bound him tight for years and years. But when this is done, he will go to Marnie in the Bad Dog Park and tell her he loves her and that he wants to wake up with her, in his bed and hers, or in a bed far away, somewhere else, just the two of them, for a month or two, or three or more.

Big Dreams

John Anderson Welles, or J.A., as he is more commonly known, has two personal assistants, Felicity and Fiona. They are waiting at the entrance to the seminar room, one with a mobile phone pressed to her ear, the other with a laptop open on her knees, both dressed in pencil skirts, short jackets and crisp white blouses.

'You must be Sylvie,' F1 says, closing her computer with a smart click. She holds out a slender hand, adorned with a simple diamond engagement ring. 'J.A. isn't far off.'

'He's taking a stroll,' F2 says, pointing to a man-made lake in the distance; it shimmers pale and still through the circle of bare birch trees. 'It's what he does. Before any event,' she explains.

Sylvie suggests that she might get herself 'set up'. She nods at the door behind them. 'Before the crowds arrive.'

'It's all done,' F1 says. 'J.A. likes us here early to make sure everything is in place.'

They are right. Chairs have been put out in neat rows, and there is a table with two piles of books: her own newly published novel alongside J.A.'s latest, simple one-liners with humorous photographs of babies' expressions to match the text. Behind the table there are boxes, filled with *From the Mouths of Babes*, and she wonders at his optimism. It is unlikely, she thinks, that a university audience will buy his work, but then who knows?

At the front of the room is a microphone on a stand.

'For you,' F1 says. 'J.A. never uses one. He likes to move around the room.'

And behind the microphone is a banner, with *So, you want to write?* across it and an image of another baby, this one sitting back in a chair, expression thoughtful, one hand rubbing its chin, the other poised above a keyboard.

Sylvie has pamphlets from the Writers' Society with her, but as she goes to place them on the empty seats, she discovers this, too, has already been taken care of.

'It seems there's nothing for me to do,' she says, and she glances at the clock on the wall, which tells her there is still half an hour to go. 'Perhaps I should have a stroll as well?'

This is not a good idea. J.A. likes to be alone on his walks.

He is due to finish in ten minutes, F2 promises.

'I might get myself a water and something to eat then,'

Sylvie says, because she is hungry. There was no time for breakfast this morning. Her son has a cold and woke several times during the night. She felt as though she had only just settled in to a deep sleep when the alarm cut through the quiet: she flicked it off immediately, dozing past the time she should have got up, leaving only a few minutes to get herself showered and dressed. She gave him Panadol, hoping it would last to when she would be back to pick him up from the centre. And then, after dropping him off, she sat in the warmth of her car, the sunshine through the windscreen causing her to close her eyes, uncertain as to whether she should try to sleep or cry, knowing she ran the risk of being late if she chose to do either.

Now that she is here, with time to kill, she wishes she had tried to rest after all.

F2 offers to come with her to the canteen. She needs to buy J.A.'s lunch.

'I can get him something,' Sylvie says, but F2 tells her it's fine.

'I know what he likes,' she explains.

It's protein. After midday, that's all J.A. eats, and F2 panics slightly as she realises it's not going to be so easy to come by in a university cafeteria.

'You could try the sushi,' Sylvie suggests.

The rice is a problem.

'He could just take it off himself, I guess.' F2 is anxious. Time is running out. A decision needs to be made. Eventually she sighs and piles four of the sushi packs in front of the register. Sylvie has ordered hot chips and a lemonade.

'Together?' the woman asks.

'Separate,' F2 says. 'With a receipt,' and she taps the plastic on the top box with a perfectly manicured fingernail.

'Have you worked for him for long?' Sylvie can't quite bring herself to say 'J.A.' out loud. In any event, her question is mumbled as she tries to eat as many of the chips as she can before they return to the room, ashamed that her attempt to finish is purely to avoid feeling embarrassed by her choice of food. She offers F2 the bucket, her fingers greasy and salty.

F2 declines. 'This is my first year,' she says. 'Fiona has been with him for three.'

'And you like the job?' She is foolish in hoping for a conspiratorial moment.

'J.A.'s wonderful,' F2 tells her. 'There's never a dull minute. You know he was on the 100 Richest Men list in the latest *Business Review Weekly*? It's the first time a writer has made it. He's very proud.'

Sylvie crushes the lemonade can in her fist and aims it for the nearest bin, the clatter of aluminium ringing out as it bounces to the bottom. She follows with the chip bucket, wiping the grease from her hands onto the side of her jeans as she hurries to catch up with F2, who is talking on her phone. It is F1. J.A. is waiting for his lunch, F2 explains; and with the sushi boxes stacked on top of one another, F2 picks up the pace, not stumbling once despite her heels, which have the frailty of needles.

J.A.'s donation of $100,000 to the Writers' Society had only one condition. He wanted a Society member to come to each of the talks he was giving to university students across the country. It wasn't a condition as such, he explained. Access to an audience of potential members was more akin to an extra gift.

'What's he getting out of it?' Sylvie had asked when the Society had rung to see whether she would do one of the events.

'He wants to be taken seriously,' Hamish, the executive director explained. 'He's angling for a spot on the board, so that people will think he's a proper writer.'

Sylvie rolled her eyes. 'Takes more than that.'

This is her third novel, and although it has only been available in the shops for a week, she can already feel it beginning to plummet. There have been no reviews, only a few requests for interviews with local papers and country radio stations, and in two of the bookshops she has been into, it has already begun to slink its way to the back shelves.

She tries to joke her way out of the despair she feels, but in her bleaker solitary moments she knows the failure of this book is likely to signal the end of her publishing career.

'Why on earth does he need to be taken seriously?' she had asked Hamish. 'He's got the sales.' The slight rasp in her voice did little to hide her envy.

Despite being certain she will not like him, Sylvie is still nervous at the prospect of meeting J.A., and this irritates her.

He is in the seminar room when they return, his back to the couple of audience members who have arrived early, his gaze fixed on the neat sweep of university grounds, as he stretches his arms overhead and limbers up.

His handshake is firm as F2 introduces them, discreetly placing the sushi boxes on the book table.

'It's so good of you to do this for the Writers' Society,' Sylvie says, her palm aching from the pressure of his grip.

He tells her it's nothing. He wants to give back. He knows how important effective networks are from all the years in which he struggled, living on nothing but hope.

Sylvie tries to nod convincingly.

J.A. glances at his sushi and grimaces. 'God, I can't bear this pre-packaged stuff.' He picks at a piece, holding it between thick fingers as he examines it, and then puts the whole lot in his mouth. A grain of rice falls onto his navy cotton drill jacket, and he flicks it off impatiently.

'Country Road,' he tells Sylvie, although she hadn't asked. 'They sponsor me — dress me from head to toe.' His teeth are startling white when he smiles.

Sylvie finds herself trying to picture him naked. It has been so many years since she has had sex with anyone that this has become an alarming habit with all new men she meets, one that usually leaves her blushing as she attempts to continue a conversation. J.A. must be at least six foot three, broad-shouldered and manly, with a square jaw, an even tan and thick dark hair. The thought of him without clothes is a disturbing one, Sylvie realises, because she has never actually slept with a manly man, and she winces at the memory of some of the more sensitive types who have found their way into her bed.

J.A. is asking her whether Felicity or Fiona has gone through the running order, and Sylvie nods, before correcting herself. She will go first, J.A. tells her. If she could explain what the Society does and introduce him — he gives her a sheet with his biographical details, and as their hands touch, Sylvie notes again how warm his skin is — he'll then speak for about thirty minutes.

'And then questions, and last — the book signings.' He waves in the direction of the boxes stacked by the table, and reaches over to pick up a copy of her novel.

'*One of the most talented writers of her generation,*' he reads from the shout line, and puts it down again.

Sylvie laughs. 'They'll say anything for a few sales.'

The audience has started to arrive, and it seems the room is going to be full. When Sylvie makes a self-deprecatory comment about not being able to remember the last time she had more than ten people show up, J.A. wanders back to the window: he hasn't been listening. Her eyes rest on his back, the firm plant of his legs in khaki cotton pants, and then run down to his leather loafers.

The little she knows about him she has gleaned only after being asked to do this event. A week ago, she read in the social pages that his engagement had been called off. There was a picture of him with a tall, willowy brunette, both arm in arm as they gazed at each other. According to the columnist, J.A. had bought a remote country estate that was to be their home after the wedding. Rumour had it she panicked when she gathered he was serious about leaving the city and living with her in isolation. As Sylvie stared at the photograph of lush hills, a two-storey sandstone house visible in the distance, she wondered what she would give up for money.

F1 and F2 are directing the last arrivals to the few empty seats left, and F2 nods at Sylvie. It is time to begin. Realising she will have to introduce herself, Sylvie stands, her mouth dry as she suddenly takes in the size of the crowd, and wishes she had prepared notes. She is brief, letting everyone know that the information about the Society is on the leaflet, and encouraging them all to join. She is about to sit down when she sees F2 nodding at her again, with even greater urgency than before. Sylvie is perplexed as F2 holds up a sheet of paper: the biog — of course, she is meant to introduce J.A. She apologises as she heads back to the stage and reads out the information he has given her.

Laughing good-naturedly, J.A. steps onto the podium

and thanks her as he rubs his hands together and then holds them up, palms towards the audience, fingers spread in a gesture of complete surprise.

'Who would have thought?' His voice booms across the room. Everyone sits up immediately.

'All those years ago, when I toiled away in a rat-infested room above Central Station, a room where the cockroaches were even bigger than the rats, with only a dream to keep me going, who would have thought?'

There are no rooms above Central Station, Sylvie thinks, and her eyes narrow in disbelief.

'More than ten million book sales in the last decade.' J.A. pauses, and the audience waits. 'Publishing deals in more than thirty countries.'

Outside a bird squawks.

'And do you know what got me here?'

One gimmicky little idea that somehow took off. Sylvie stares at the ground.

'Courage. You might think that seems a strong word to apply to something so genteel as writing. But let me tell you what I know about courage. When I was in my early twenties I joined the army. They taught us about courage there, particularly in the division I belonged to. We were an elite crack team. Trained to respond without fear in situations that would have most of us,' and he waves his hand around the room, 'curled up and crying in the corner. So I learnt about courage. Or at least I thought I had. Because in the years that followed, when I was in that room above Central Station, trying not to fall apart from the despair and the loneliness and the rejection — well, that was when I had to call upon all my reserves of strength.

'Shall I tell you about my rejections?'

No one responds, but they are all listening, eager for him to continue.

'I kept every one of those letters. And there were over three hundred of them. I stuck them up on the toilet wall, I covered every inch of space.'

Surely not, Sylvie thinks. She has heard this story before. It's standard writers' fare, so clichéd no one would dare use it.

'And each time I sat in there, doing what we all do in a bathroom, I re-read them. Not as some sort of punishment, but because I knew' — he pauses here — 'what doesn't kill us only makes us stronger.'

He smiles, those even teeth white and strong, and the audience laughs, appreciatively.

He believes it, Sylvie realises. He actually believes what he says.

'Even in the worst times, the times when I had nothing to eat, no friends — except the cockroaches and the rats — and no way of paying the rent, I hung on to that faith, and I didn't give up.

'Shall I tell you about my break?'

As he continues with his anecdotes, finally winding up with a PowerPoint guide on how to fulfil your dream,

Sylvie moves beyond wondering what he would be like naked to what he would be like as a lover. Perfunctory? Imaginative? She finds that one hard to believe. Selfish? He is probably depressive, she thinks. People who swallow the kind of crap he does usually are. She wants to remove the various images that are appearing, but she also finds them strangely fascinating.

'Questions?' J.A. asks, and the hands shoot up. The first few he answers happily: they are questions about his success, his sales, his publishing deals, what he plans to do next. The fourth, however, is a different kettle of fish.

The woman is near the back. She wears coral lipstick and a plum-coloured velour tracksuit. Her make-up is heavy, failing to disguise the fact that she is nearer seventy than sixty, and her hair needs re-dyeing, the grey roots making the blonde tips even brassier.

'I wrote a book,' she says.

J.A. brushes the sleeve of his cotton jacket.

'And it was a good book. My family said so. And my friends.'

Sensing trouble, F1 and F2 are sitting upright in their seats.

'I sent it to every publisher and they rejected it.'

J.A. nods sympathetically. He understands, he tells her. She mustn't give up.

But no, that is not her point, and she interrupts him.

'Now,' she tells him, 'one of them has just put out another book and it's a copy of mine.'

'What do you mean, it's a copy of yours?' J.A. has moved to the window and he rests against the sill, half glancing out at the smooth lawns and pale sky.

'A copy,' the woman insists. 'That's just what I mean. And when I contact them, they don't return my calls. They won't have anything to do with me.'

'What is your question?'

The woman is getting frustrated. 'I want to know what I can do. How I can stop these crooks from stealing my intellectual property. How I can get justice.'

'Have you been to a lawyer?' J.A. asks.

'I can't afford a lawyer.' The woman pokes her finger in the air, and her voice grates like metal on metal.

J.A. is silent, and Sylvie wonders whether she is going to see him rattled. She watches, curious. Then, surprisingly, he turns to her and smiles. She gives him a look of sympathy to let him know that, like all writers, she has had her fair share of mad audience members.

The pause is brief. J.A. is once again in command. 'I think this is a question that I should pass over.' J.A. nods in Sylvie's direction. 'As a representative of the Writers' Society, our guest is considerably more qualified to answer than I am.'

Sylvie shifts in her seat. She clears her throat. She has had no sleep.

J.A. has turned to the window and is not even pretending to hold any interest in what she is going to say.

The microphone is now off and her voice is faint, pathetic, as she fails to make one of the many responses she would like to make, but instead tells the woman that the Society has a legal officer who would be happy to assist.

'I've contacted them,' the woman says, arms folded across her ample breasts.

'And they couldn't help?'

'They fobbed me off.'

'Well, without knowing further details, I can't make a comment on that.'

'I'll give you further details.' The woman steps forward and waves a bundle of papers in her hand. 'These are all the letters I sent and the replies. Here.' She starts walking down the aisle towards Sylvie, who steps back, accidentally treading on J.A.'s foot.

'I'm not sure what I can do with these,' Sylvie protests. 'I'm sorry.'

'You can give me an answer. They can't go doing what they've done. Stealing my property like that and not paying me a penny.'

It is not until the woman has one foot on the podium that J.A. intervenes. His large hand resting on her shoulder, he tells her that he sympathises with her plight but this isn't the forum. He and Sylvie would be more than happy to chat to her further after the book signings at the end, although there may not be much they can actually do.

There is a certain resonance in his voice, a depth to the timbre that, combined with the solidity of his large hand, is designed to lull. Like a stun gun.

It is so effective that Sylvie imagines the relief of telling him all her own problems. He would place his hand on her shoulder, the very weight of it making her and her difficulties seem slight. This is what I am. Why struggle?

Blinking, she watches as the woman walks back to the audience, docile now. J.A. resumes his place at the front of the room. Standing awkwardly by his side, Sylvie is aware that she may be the only one to come out of this fiasco appearing like the fool. She takes her seat and stares down at her lap, while J.A. wraps up proceedings.

Shortly after she agreed to do this session, a friend of Sylvie's told her that he had once met J.A. at a charity function. It was a black-tie event to raise money for cystic fibrosis. Sylvie's friend, Bobby, had been a waiter. At the end of the evening, J.A. was sitting alone at one of the tables, surrounded by empty wineglasses, staring out at the last few drunks, lurching towards one another in dishevelled suits and dresses that had gone askew. Was he alright? Bobby had asked as he cleared the glasses.

See that woman? J.A. had pointed to a bare-limbed woman in a sliver of fabric. *She is my fiancée.*

Bobby had congratulated J.A. and made a move towards the next table, but J.A. stopped him.

Have you ever been in love?

Bobby told J.A. that he fell in love with nearly every man he met, and then, sensing a spark through the cloak of alcohol, he'd gone on to tell J.A. he was finishing his shift and heading out, if he was interested.

'And he joined you, of course?' Sylvie was tired of all her gay friends boasting of their successful conquests.

'He wanted it.'

J.A. had taken Bobby by the arm. He had pulled him down to sit and he had offered him a drink.

Look at her. J.A. pointed to where his fiancée leant against the wall, one leg crossed over the other, hands clutched around a bottle of champagne as she talked to an older man. *She is the person I'm marrying.*

Bobby had slipped J.A. an E. *Take this*, he instructed, *and meet me out the back in half an hour.*

'It was a waste. He was so drunk he dropped it on the floor and trod on it.' Bobby had rolled his eyes in disgust.

But it was not the end of his story.

Later, after the glasses were cleared and he had emerged from the hall, all the lights turned on to dispel the last few stragglers, he had seen J.A. again. Standing solemn, silent, 'like a tree trunk — a very handsome tree trunk, but a tree trunk all the same', with his fiancée and the man she had been talking to. J.A. didn't say a word, while the other two were animated, engaging in an urgent tumble of conversation in which J.A. refused to participate, despite their best efforts. Eventually, the fiancée stopped. She took J.A.'s hand, kissed him on the cheek, and got into a cab with the other man. And still he didn't move.

'I mean, that is strange behaviour,' Bobby had said.

He hesitated but then walked up to J.A. — 'there was no harm in one last try' — and told him the offer was still open if he was interested.

'And you know what he did?'

Sylvie didn't.

'He took my face in his hands — big hands — and then he pulled me close and he kissed me. Tongues and all!'

'He did not.' Sylvie laughed.

Her friend grinned. 'Wish he had. But, no. He just looked at me like he had no idea who I was and then turned and walked away by himself.'

Sylvie remembers this story as F1 shepherds her towards the book-signing table. The queue started forming as soon as J.A. finished talking, and in less than a minute there is already a snaking line of people, reaching the exit door.

'That was brilliant,' F1 says, referring to the session.

Sylvie tries to seem enthused. 'Apart from that lunatic.'

But F1 just looks quizzical, as though the mad woman and her stolen manuscript never existed. She pulls out a seat for Sylvie, and it is only as Sylvie sits that she realises there is not a single person waiting to have her sign a copy of her book, whereas the queue for J.A.

has now gone into the corridor.

She watches them, one by one, clutching their copy of *From the Mouths of Babes*, as they stand before J.A. and tell him how much they love his work.

'I gave it to my sister when she had cancer and it got her through chemo.'

'I bought a copy for my teenage daughter — and I swear it made her a little less difficult.'

'I read a quote a day and try to live by it.'

J.A. acknowledges each of them, his eyes fixed on theirs, his hand often clasping theirs just for an instant.

After what feels like five minutes but is probably a lot less, Sylvie decides she doesn't need to inflict this on herself any longer. Her bag is on the floor at her feet, and she makes a show of rummaging through it until she finds her phone.

In the brief break between readers, she tells J.A. she has to leave.

'I'm terribly sorry, but the person minding my son has just texted. He has an ear infection.' She lies without blinking.

J.A. puts down his pen and excuses himself from the woman who waits, book in hand, for his signature. He turns to Sylvie, and it is the first time she feels that he is actually seeing her.

'I didn't know you had a son.'

Sylvie nods.

'Lucky you.'

'I know.' She meets his gaze. 'Even though I'm on my own and sometimes it's hard, I still wouldn't change a thing.'

J.A. reaches into the pocket of his jacket and gives her a card. 'If you ever need anything,' he says as she gets up to leave.

And she thanks him.

Later that evening, she sits, legs up on the couch, and starts on her third glass of wine. She lives in a ground-floor flat with windows over a small common garden, overgrown with sweet william, tiny pink-and-white flowers that she would like to rip out and replace with something more substantial. The curtains are still open and the night is black, the room lit by a single wooden lamp that gives off an orange glow. The floor is littered with Lex's trucks, games, plastic stacking cups and an old wooden stove with a fried egg in a pan and a chipped enamel kettle on top. She used to put all his toys in the corner each night, giving herself a few hours in which she could pretend she had some room in the intensity of their relationship. It was a pretence that dissolved as soon as she went to bed, Lex lying in his cot next to her and not in his own room because she wanted to try to keep the other bedroom as an office, although she knows this will soon have to go.

The couch is covered in an old moss-green cord, a colour she likes, although it is a little worn. On the wooden floor is a Persian rug that belonged to her mother, the deep red capable of hiding all stains. The table is littered with the newspaper and the remnants of her evening meal. She will clear it soon. For now, she just wants to sit and drink her glass of wine.

It is a pleasant apartment, but she knows she spends too much time here. She is either caring for Lex or writing, both of which take place within these rooms. She occasionally has people over, although not often. She rarely goes out because she can't afford it. All she is has narrowed down to this, a tightly confined existence that could conceivably remain this way for far longer than she would like.

In her hands she holds the card that J.A. gave her as she left, and she turns it over and over, a simple black card with two words written on the front: *BIG DREAMS*. His name, the address of the studio where he produces his books, and his mobile number are on the back.

She contemplates what it would be like to call him, and to suggest they meet for a coffee. She sees him, tall, square-jawed, dressed in smart casuals, pants pleated at the front, loafers, those white, straight teeth, and she envisages sitting opposite him and trying to converse. She cannot imagine how he would even fit into her lounge room.

She puts her wineglass down and finds herself giggling.

And then, just as she is about to carry her plate to

the kitchen, she stops and picks up the phone. Without thinking, she begins to dial the numbers, one after the other, wanting only to act in a way that is completely unexpected.

J.A.? she will say. It's me, Sylvie.

As she tries to imagine where she would go from there, she is greeted by the sound of his voice, the timbre unmistakable, and she twists the cord tight around her finger while she hovers, caught in a space that cannot last, mouth open ready to speak, hand poised, ready to hang up, floundering as he asks her who's calling and she stumbles to say her name.

The Other Side of the River

David had the address scribbled in the margin of an article he wanted to finish reading in the car. Ellen didn't know the suburb. The name was familiar — one of those roads that stretched for miles, sometimes a main artery, at other times dwindling into little more than a street.

'You're going to have to direct me,' she told him, and he sighed as he folded up the paper and pulled out the street directory.

'I wish we didn't even have to go,' she said, glancing at herself in the rear-vision mirror.

'Me, too,' Evie agreed from the back seat, and Ellen winked at her.

'At least you'll have a friend there,' Ellen said, as she turned the key in the ignition.

'Sienna is not my friend,' Evie said. 'We're not even in the same class.'

GEORGIA BLAIN

It was midwinter and dark already. The road was busy, a line of cars, white headlights beaming as they inched their way home. Ellen turned the heater up, the rush of air stale and gritty, but warm on her feet as they edged out into the traffic, heading south over the river.

'You just follow this road forever,' David said, before turning back to his article.

If they were staying home tonight, she thought, David would have made minestrone, or a pasta. Unlike her, he enjoyed cooking. The three of them would have eaten it in front of the television, blinds down, gas heater on. After dinner, when Evie went to bed, she would have gone back up to her studio to add the next layer to the piece she was working on, or maybe she would have let it rest tonight, lying on the couch with David instead, watching a movie. He had his head bent low, still attempting to read in the dimness of the car light.

A few metres on, the road diverged and she didn't know which branch to take. 'You're meant to be navigating,' she said as she pulled over, and David looked guiltily at the map. He traced the line and told her she had to go back.

'I need you to watch for the house numbers,' she said when they were on the right road, traffic thinning, neat suburban bungalows lining each side of what had become a wide street.

'That's 420,' Evie called out.

'So it can't be far now.' Ellen leant closer to the

110

windscreen, trying to make out the digits on the low brick walls or the front doors with 1940s portholes. It was going to be a matter of counting, she decided, and as they drew near to what must be 522, she turned to David and rolled her eyes.

'In and out,' she said.

He shrugged helplessly. 'What could I say?'

When David had picked Evie up from school two days ago, Matthew had asked them all over for dinner.

'Why us?'

'I don't know.' David had seemed as dismayed as her. 'I guess he's lonely. And he knows me vaguely through the paper.'

Ellen had only recently noticed Matthew in the playground. She had never spoken to him, although she had talked twice to Cath, his ex-partner. They all waited together under the shade of the few wattles that grew in the schoolyard, mothers and fathers, sometimes making conversation, sometimes choosing to sit apart until the bell rang.

Like Ellen, Cath often sat on her own. Ellen would try to hold on to these last minutes of being alone, moments to work out a technical problem, or a question of surface that had been plaguing her. She only talked to Cath because she happened to glance over, and saw she had her arm in plaster.

'How did you do that?' Ellen had asked politely. She

had been expecting an ordinary answer — in fact, she hadn't even really wanted to know — so she was surprised when Cath had turned away sharply, wiping at her eyes.

Ellen muttered an apology, coupled with an attempt at reassurance, hoping the bell would ring soon. It did.

The next time she saw her, Cath said she was sorry. 'About the tears,' and nodded at her arm.

It was fine, Ellen had told her, but Cath interrupted: 'I've been splitting up with Matthew, Sienna's father.' Her words were blunt, as though she were daring herself to utter them without crying.

Ellen didn't know what to say.

'It's a good thing,' Cath said. 'Ultimately.'

They were engulfed by a swarm of children, Evie pulling on Ellen's sleeve as she held up her merit certificate. But as they walked outside the school gates, Ellen saw Cath again, holding Sienna's hand and heading down the hill towards the river.

'Do you reckon you'd ever want to have Sienna over to play?'

'No,' Evie replied.

That night Ellen mentioned the conversation to David. They were sitting out the back of the house, enjoying the last warmth of a late-summer evening.

'I wonder whether he broke her arm.' She said the words idly, slapping at a mosquito as she did so.

'That's something of a leap.' David finished his beer and turned to go into the kitchen.

Ellen felt ashamed, which only made her continue. 'There's something about him I don't like,' she said. 'He's so …' She searched for the word. 'Masculine.'

'Masculinity doesn't make someone a wife basher.' David shut the door behind him, leaving Ellen outside alone. *I know*, she wanted to say, but then she couldn't be bothered.

Later that evening she stood at the entrance to her studio, one hand on the light switch. She had been working on a sphere, painstakingly created from leaves and twigs pinned together, the inner structure built from fallen branches. Under the overhead globe, it looked dead, the range of colour fading into a single dull brown, brittle to the touch. Sitting on the floor with her back against the doorframe, she glanced down to the house. David was in the kitchen, putting away the remains of the meal. Beyond was darkness: the room where Evie slept and, at the front, their own room. She rolled a cigarette from the secret supply of tobacco that she kept stashed at the bottom of her filing cabinet. The match flared too bright, dying as suddenly as it had come to life.

She had been with David for twelve years now. He was, she often told people, the only man she had ever loved. They had met when she was at art school and he was in his second year as a journalist. He reviewed her final-year show, picking her work as the most promising. At an exhibition about a month later, they were introduced and she asked him out. He was seeing someone, and it wasn't really appropriate — people would think he had given her such a good write-up because he was sleeping with her. She didn't know whether he was serious or not, but she didn't give in. They drank until closing time.

At four in the morning, he was telling her about growing up in a country town and wanting to be a guitar player in a band. He spent a year hitchhiking his way around Australia before he settled in Sydney. She had never left anything or gone anywhere, she said. She now lived only two streets from where she had grown up with parents who had always let her do as she pleased. And then she remembered she had completed four years of architecture before she realised it wasn't what she wanted. 'So I guess I left that,' and she tried to stand, giggling at her poor balance. He helped her up, pulling her in as he did so, and they kissed. It was like perfection, she thought. Sweet, essential. She had told him that she adored him.

The light in the studio was bad, but she had an idea, a change in colour gradation to bring the work back to life. She began to unpick a fine line of leaves across the sphere, leaving her cigarette burning out on the edge of the step. Carefully storing the shortest twigs that held the surface together, she worked slowly, wanting the shape to be right the first time round.

Ellen slammed the car door shut behind her. A white gum stretched up into the darkness, its limbs smooth and pale, bent and graceful, as it swayed, silvery leaves shivering.

'Look,' she said, and David and Evie turned to glance up at the tree, remarkable for its survival along a road that boasted no more than the occasional grevillea or bottlebrush, and even more extraordinary for its singular beauty.

David stepped back, and she could see that he, too, found the tree worth stopping for. He took her hand in his.

'I could cope with living out here,' Ellen said, 'with a tree like that.' She uttered the words more to herself than to the others. As she started to walk through the low iron gateway, Evie stopped her.

'It's not that place,' she said. 'It's there,' and she pointed further up the road.

David knocked on the door and Sienna opened it, peering out at the three of them. She was a small child, thin limbs, straight hair in two tight pigtails, and dark eyes.

'Hi, Evie,' she muttered, when behind her Matthew bent down to whisper in her ear, his instruction to say hello audible to all of them.

'Hi.' Evie kept her eyes fixed on the ground, pressing backwards into Ellen.

Inside, they stood too close in the hallway, until Matthew led them through to a sunroom off the kitchen, where a table had been set, with five mismatched chairs drawn up. Ellen could hear the faint hum of a cello concerto in the background, and she found the stereo next to her, on top of the pine bookshelves. She ran her finger along the titles while, from the kitchen, Matthew asked if they wanted a drink. There were books of poetry, and this surprised her. She pulled one of the paperbacks out, only to hastily replace it as she heard Matthew coming to give her a glass of white.

'I discovered Gerard Manley Hopkins when I was at university.' He brushed by her as he took the book out once more, the cover dog-eared, the pages yellowing. 'His angst spoke to me, but more than anything it was what he did with language. Turning it on its head. Stirring up years of soft romanticism with harshness and vigour.'

Ellen asked him if it was true that Hopkins was gay.

'There was a school of criticism that emphasised the possibility.' Matthew took a careful sip of the wine, tasting it slowly.

It was, Ellen soon discovered, very dry and very good. She commented appreciatively, and he held up the bottle for them to see. It was a favourite, he said, from a tiny vineyard in the south of France. He had hunted it down from a specialist wine shop near work, giving half-a-dozen to Cath when they split up and saving the other half for himself.

'Cheers.' David held out his glass and they all clinked.

Ellen said she would check whether the children were okay. Outside Sienna's room, she could hear them talking. They were playing Monopoly, and she asked them both, a little too brightly, how the game was going. When neither of them replied, she went back to the kitchen.

David had pulled his chair out from the table, his legs extended in front of him. He had already finished his glass and was discussing a film he had seen the other night. It had been a slow-moving piece about the last day in a man's life, a film in which not much happened, although its very emptiness had a certain resonance when you knew the end.

'I can't say I enjoyed it as much as you did,' Ellen said. 'Although I'm not as anti-narrative as you are.'

Matthew turned to her. 'I'm glad to hear some people are still partial to the story. I've been writing a novel.'

She murmured something encouraging, and David asked him what it was about. 'Or are you one of those writers that hates saying?'

He wasn't. It was about a French anthropologist, a man who lived with Aboriginal people at the beginning of the twentieth century. 'He turned his back on white society and then couldn't return when he wanted. It's loosely based on a true story.' He took a large dish out of the oven, and lifted the lid briefly. 'I hope you like cassoulet?'

'Can't say I've ever had it,' David confessed, and Ellen could only admire him for his straight-faced reply. It was not a meal either of them had been expecting. The invitation, she thought, had been for a quick dinner with the kids.

'I learnt to cook it when Cath and I lived in Paris,'

Matthew told them.

'When was that?' Ellen felt obliged to ask.

'About four years ago. We took leave so I could research my book.' He looked at her. 'You've been there,' he said. 'For six months in a studio.'

She tried to conceal the surprise she felt at his knowledge of her life. 'Yes,' she answered. 'We both went before Evie was born.'

'I read it in your biog.' He began to serve up the food as he spoke. 'At your last exhibition.'

David offered to call the kids, and Ellen found herself alone with Matthew. She asked if she could help. Perhaps she could carry the plates over? He was placing each serve in the centre with perfect precision, and as she reached to take the nearest, he turned slightly to rest the ladle on the edge of the sink, his other elbow knocking her.

The plate did not shatter, but the cassoulet covered her suede boots and spread across the lino on the kitchen floor. She swore without thinking, bending down to wipe the sauce off her feet as he, too, crouched, their faces so close that she felt the warmth of his breath and the brush of his thick black hair against her cheek.

'I'm fine,' she said, stepping back as Evie and Sienna came into the room.

'Your boots will be wrecked.' Evie surveyed the damage from the doorway, and Ellen wished they had never discussed how easily suede could be marked.

Ten years later, when Evie left school, she told Ellen how much she had disliked Matthew. The year in which he had come to live with Ellen had been the worst, she said.

'I know,' Ellen said. 'I didn't like him much either.'

'Then why did you do it?'

They were sitting in the back garden, sharing a bottle of champagne and cigarettes in celebration of Evie having finished her exams. Her daughter's face was like David's, Ellen thought, taking in her pale green eyes, wide mouth, and slow smile, blurred by the late-afternoon sun and too much drink. Her temperament, too: she was even-natured, reasonable and strangely distant. Ellen considered Evie's question. It was one she used to ask herself whenever she gazed at the raw wound of missing the life she once had, flesh no longer covered by the paper-thin layer of breathless excitement. But each time she had come face to face with that question, she had quickly shied away. The answer was too difficult to find, and probably not worth the search. *I don't know*, she was about to say, but then she didn't.

'He appalled me,' she told Evie, 'and that was what I found fascinating.' She looked out across the overgrown garden, weeds creeping into each of the beds, rocket gone to seed, nasturtiums tangled sickly sweet around the base of the lemon tree.

Evie did not respond.

It was not an explanation, or at least not one her daughter would understand, just as David had found a similar attempt she had once made for him far from satisfactory. She reached across the table, about to pour them both another glass of champagne, but stopped. Opposite her, Evie was crying, silent tears that slid down her cheek, wiped away as quickly as they appeared.

'I'm sorry,' Ellen said, and she was truly sorry as she laid her own hand over Evie's. A line of ants trailed across the tabletop between them, running straight until they reached a pool of spilt drink. The branches of the giant wattle next door creaked in the breeze. She glanced up at the sun and closed her eyes, the memory of that year with Matthew still strong enough to make her shake her head, wanting to physically remove any trace of him from her life.

'I was so happy,' she said. 'With you and David. And I was making these perfect beautiful sculptures that were so complete. When total destruction knocks on your door, sometimes it's very tempting to take a look.'

Wiping the last of her tears, Evie ran a finger across the table. 'You know I saw a review for his book the other day?'

Ellen didn't.

'It was good,' Evie said. 'It even made me want to read it.'

Ellen smiled, and as she did so, she contemplated the explanation she had tried to give. It was close, she thought, but there are parts of life that evade words. There are countless choices — and you always choose to do the right thing: to drive without crashing the car, not to walk into the oncoming traffic, to stop drinking, not to say what you think.

She remembered standing just inside Matthew's bedroom, undressing him as he undressed her and knowing that a month earlier, on the night they had eaten cassoulet, she had stood outside this room, aware of how little it would take to step over into a life that repelled her, and also fascinated her. In the sunroom off the kitchen, Matthew had opened another bottle of wine, and David had relented, sitting back and letting his glass be refilled. She had sat with them, listening to their conversation, participating occasionally, only to withdraw again, her gaze turning to the dishes neatly stacked in the rack, the new fridge, and the three saucepans sitting on top of the stove. Beyond was the lounge room, the carpet floral, the walls painted a violet that had been popular in the fifties, a new television in the corner, and a cheap two-seater couch in front of it.

She had got up to go to the bathroom, wanting to look. Inside the cupboard there was a razor, soap, toothbrush and toothpaste, and a packet of Panadol. She had stood for a moment, leaning against the shower screen. In the room next door, the girls were talking about school. Sienna was asking Evie which of the boys she liked and Evie was being evasive. 'All of them,' she answered. 'It's wrong not to like everyone.'

As she stepped out into the hall, she could see

Matthew's room at the end of the corridor. The blind was drawn, but the bed was visible, neatly made, with four pillows at one end, a bedside table on one side only, and on it two books and a white metal light clipped to the edge.

'I think I need to get going,' she had told David when she sat back down in the sunroom.

He was remembering the editor of the paper when he had first joined. 'He was completely straight. Middle-aged — well, probably the same as we are now — suit, tie, neat hair, very traditional, apart from the fact that he meditated. For half an hour every lunchtime. He would just shut the door and sit there, eyes closed. Everyone knew what he was doing, and not to disturb him, and no one ever mentioned it. But it was bloody strange. I mean, it was so unexpected from him.' David topped up his glass. 'He was the calmest, easiest boss I've ever had.'

'I have to go,' she said again, knowing she was going to be ignored.

But Matthew heard her. 'You don't look well.' He was staring right at her, his eyes dark and still, intent and focused.

'I'm just tired,' she said. 'I have another show soon and I've been working long hours.'

'I know,' Matthew said. 'It's at Gallery 4. I've been looking forward to it.'

In the car on the way home, she had asked David why he never listened to her, why they had to stay so long, it was insufferable, awful; and he had looked in the rear-vision mirror to where Evie was sitting, listening to everything they were saying.

'Why was it awful?' Evie had asked. 'Didn't you like Sienna's dad?'

'No,' Ellen had lied. 'I did like him.'

'He certainly knew your form.'

Ellen glanced sharply at David, who grinned back at her.

At home, David took Evie straight to bed, dressing her in her pyjamas, while Ellen switched on the heaters.

'She can't wear summer pyjamas,' she said when she came in to kiss Evie goodnight.

'It doesn't matter,' David said.

'It does,' and Ellen began to unbutton the top, pushing David to one side.

'Don't be ridiculous.' He refused to move. 'You're just going to get her cold if you undress her again.'

'I'm fine,' Evie said, pulling the doona up over her chest.

'You're not,' Ellen insisted, forcing the covers down. She could feel David's arm on her wrist, holding her back, and she shook herself free. 'Leave me alone.'

'No, leave her alone,' he said. 'Let her go to sleep.'

But Ellen wouldn't. With the flannel pyjamas under one arm, she continued to try to undress Evie, who kept saying that she was okay. It was only when David forced her away that she stopped, and she turned to shout at him, her mouth open and ready, only silencing herself as she realised where they both were. But outside in the hall, she hissed: 'Why do you have to fight me?'

'I don't,' he had said, perplexed.

Now, so many years later, she and David speak occasionally and have dinner together less often, sometimes at his house, sometimes at hers. They talk about Evie, or work, or friends they have in common, and then they clear the table, and one washes while the other dries. It is almost as it should be, close to the way it might have been if she had never made that one particular choice. She opened the door, she thinks. She had a look.

Escape

My father liked to think of himself as an intellectual, a tad bohemian, handsome, a bon vivant and a raconteur. All admirable traits, but perhaps not so essential for the job of parenting — one that he managed to avoid for most of the year and then was forced to embrace each summer holiday.

He picked us up in his frog-green Porsche Roadster, the engine throbbing in our suburban street. The fact that there would barely be enough room for our suitcases never occurred to him, let alone the problem of how we would fit into a car that didn't have a back seat.

'Both of you in the front,' he would say, and my sister and I would squash, awkward and embarrassed, into the tiny leather bucket seat, straining to wrap the belt around our bodies.

Our mother stayed inside for our departure, telling us

she'd prefer to stare at the ceiling and pray we'd get there alive than witness his driving.

'And off we go!' Foot to the floor, gears sliding smoothly into place, the wind in our hair, Pink Floyd booming on the stereo, we were headed out of 'Dullsville' (my father's word) and off to the land of pot, lissom young women, meals when you felt like it, and six weeks of parental neglect.

Sass was thirteen that summer, and I was twelve. She rarely spoke to us anymore, hiding in her room as soon as she got home from school, listening to records and reading books. I missed her, and didn't understand why she had withdrawn.

'Good god, you're a woman,' my father said when we arrived at his house.

She glared at him and then picked up her case and walked on ahead of us.

My father's house was a low-lying brick-and-timber building with more windows than walls, built alongside similar houses, each hidden from the next by tangled bush. There was no garden, just scrub: callistemon, hop bush, gold-dust wattle and yellow box, all pressed tight against each other, leaving no space to play, no lawn.

'*Lawn belongs in Dullsville.*' My mother would imitate my father when I complained about having nothing to do there — no backyard cricket, nowhere to kick the football. '*Don't tell me you belong in Dullsville, too.*' She would roll her eyes. It was only six weeks: I had to grin and bear it, and before I knew it I'd be back in the suburbs in my dull house with my dull mother.

Usually Sass and I slept in the den, a box-like room that faced south, our camp beds side by side, one end wedged in under our father's desk, every surface covered in papers, books and recording equipment — headphones, a Nagra and several microphones — as well as metal canisters containing reels of tape: interviews he did outside the studio and off-cuts from edits.

There was no reason to think there would be any change to our accommodation, and our father certainly hadn't mentioned that he had another guest — not that we would have been able to hear anything in the car should he have taken the unusual step of attempting a conversation with us.

But the room was different. Everything had a place in the shelves, and there was a neatly made single bed in the corner. We might have thought he'd gone to some effort if it wasn't for how unlikely that would be, and the presence of only one bed also indicated otherwise.

'Jen!' My father's voice echoed down the hall, bouncing off the bare boards and the many windows. 'Jen! Your charges have arrived!' He had his arms around us, and I could smell him, the garlic he must have eaten for lunch pungent as he pulled me closer than I liked.

Sass had already stepped out of his grasp, and she stood there, case at her feet, arms folded, taking in the slender girl (who didn't seem much older than she was) at the entrance to the kitchen.

'Gidday.'

Her accent was strange.

She held out her hand. 'Sass? Patrick?'

I attempted one of my father's handshakes, firm and manly. Sass just gave her one of my mother's best death stares.

Introductions done, my father removed his arm, intending to head straight out the door.

'Where are you going?' I said.

'Work to do.' He winked at us and reached over to ruffle my hair. 'See you this evening.'

Jen was from New Zealand. She told me this on our third day, when I had once again failed to understand what she was saying.

'Christchurch.'

'We're atheists,' I said, my mouth full of sandwich.

'You are so embarrassing.' Sass glared at me, her voice a low hiss. 'It's a city.'

I refused to blush. 'Well, we are atheists.'

'With a father like yours, I'm not surprised.' Jen's eyes were kind.

'It's our mother,' I told her. 'She was brought up a Catholic and she hates anything to do with the church now.'

Jen was brought up a Quaker. She bit into an apple, her teeth gleaming white against the dusty gold of her skin. 'The jury is still out for me.'

'That's called agnostic,' I said. 'Dad says they're lily-livered fence-sitters.'

'Sometimes you get quite a view from the top of the fence.' She nibbled around the core. 'What about you?' She turned to Sass.

My sister shrugged. 'I guess I'm an atheist. I mean, I don't believe in heaven or hell or a god who sits up in the sky and watches everything we do. Sometimes you get caught out and punished; other times you get away scot-free.'

I stared at her. It was the most she'd said in months.

We were in the lounge room, hot and bored, the windows open to tired puffs of scorching breeze carrying dust and blowflies. We had no car to go anywhere, buses were a half-hour walk away, and the house contained only newspapers, biographies and political books.

'Let's cook,' Jen said.

Sass and I waited for more, for some enticement to lift us out of our torpor.

'A cake,' she tried. 'With as many layers as we can make.'

There was, of course, so little in the kitchen, and as she put each of the potential ingredients out on the bench, trying to find poor substitutes for essentials such as sugar, I could see her enthusiasm waning.

And then she had an idea. She sucked on the nub of a pencil before commencing a list.

'Chocolate,' Sass said. 'We need chocolate.'

She wrote it down dutifully.

'Milk,' I added. 'And eggs.'

She narrowed her eyes. 'Does butter go in cakes?'

I wasn't sure. She put it on the list anyway.

Sass opened the fridge and then shut it in disgust. 'Who's going to give us all that stuff?'

'Stephanie,' Jen said. 'My sister.'

I had to stop myself from giggling at the way she said 'sister'.

'You never told us you had a sister. Or that she lived near here.' Sass sat on a stool and dipped her finger into the jar of honey.

Jen folded up the piece of paper. 'You never asked. She's an au pair. At the Donaldsons'. I came to visit her and your dad said I could take care of you two over the summer.'

Sass decided to stay behind and read, but I offered to walk with Jen, wanting to meet this sister. We trudged up the gravel driveway towards the road, waving at the persistent flies that clustered on our sweaty skin, and trying to shade our eyes from the flat glare of the day.

It wasn't like this in New Zealand, Jen told me. It was cool and green, and it rained for days on end. Misty rain on rolling hills.

'I wish we lived there,' I said. 'I hate it here. I even like Dullsville better than this.'

She glanced at me quizzically, and I explained that it

was my father's name for our suburb. 'It might be boring,' I added, 'but at least it's not as ugly as this.' I gestured at the grey of the surrounding scrub, which scratched our legs and arms if we veered to either side of the narrow driveway.

'It has its own beauty,' Jen said. 'You mightn't see it because it's so familiar to you, but to someone like me — well, it's got something.'

I didn't notice the police car at first. It was parked off the road, half hidden by a wattle, the grille glinting in the sunlight. The windows were open and the front seat was reclined, the policeman lying back, eyes closed, mouth wide as he snored.

'He's going to swallow a lot of flies,' Jen said.

I giggled.

'He's also going to miss what he came to see. If it happens.'

I didn't understand her.

'Dickhead.'

The way she said the word, it sounded like 'duckhead'.

'Why's he here?' I asked.

She contemplated my question. A fly settled on the tip of her nose and she brushed it away. Scraping her hair back in a ponytail, which she knotted at the nape of her neck, she kept her eyes locked on mine as she tried to think of the best way to answer.

'Okay,' she said. 'It's like this: there's a man and he's called Les.'

I waited for her to continue.

'He's escaped from jail.'

'Is he near here?' The alarm in my voice made an embarrassing squeak.

She didn't answer straightaway. Overhead the sun was burning fiercely, a white-hot halo bleaching colour out of the day.

'Stephanie is his girlfriend,' she said at last. 'The police think he might try and visit her.'

A magpie watched us from the branch of a river red gum, its talons gripped around the sheaves of rust-coloured bark, the sharp glitter of its eyes observing our progress.

'What'd he do?' I hardly dared ask the question.

She'd been expecting it. 'I thought you'd want to know. Everyone does.' We turned right into another driveway similar to my father's, although a little more kempt. She was staring straight ahead as she said the words. 'It was armed robbery.'

I can only assume my intake of air was audible. I felt sweat on my forehead, damp and cold, and I wiped it away.

'Your dad knows him.'

I had no idea.

'He's been interviewing him. He's making a program about him and life in prison.' She flicked a piece of dry grass off her arm. 'It's all top secret. Les calls with a number and then your father rings him, and they make a time and a place.'

'Have you met him?'

She hadn't. 'But Steph loves him —' The driveway turned in front of us to reveal a house, so like my father's, canary-yellow door wide open, the sound of children screaming inside. She beckoned me to follow, her last words ('— and that's enough for me') swallowed by a howl as a girl, who could have been no more than four, tripped and fell, bone cracking hard on the slate floor.

Jen scooped her up. 'Rosie, Rosie, Rose.' She danced her round until she was sufficiently distracted, the watery smile on her face gradually dissolving into peals of laughter.

'Steph,' Jen called out, and an identical young woman came out of the kitchen, carrying a baby, his nose dripping with snot.

I turned from one to the other, and then back again.

Jen winked at me. 'Forgot to tell you we're twins.'

The kitchen was chaos — kids' toys scattered across the floor; cereal bowls with dried food on the table and flies buzzing around them; a milk bottle open, the smell sour and thick.

'Police still there?' Steph asked, putting the boy on the ground, where he began to bang a wooden block on the quarry tiles.

Jen nodded.

Steph sniffed, breathing in deeply before she spoke, her voice little more than a whisper. 'I wish they'd leave.'

The little boy crawled across the floor and pulled

himself up by holding on to her leg. She reached down for him, an action that was automatic and worn out, her hip adjusting to his weight, her slow movement soothing him.

The young girl, Rosie, pulled at my hand. 'Come and see my room,' she demanded. I wanted to stay where I was, listening to their conversation. Finding out about Les was the only interesting thing that had happened this summer and I didn't want to miss a second of it.

'It's been two days since he's called,' Steph said.

Rosie continued to insist on my attention, standing up now and using all of her body to try to pull me up, too. 'Come on,' she said, over and over again, and I gave in.

Later, as we headed home, I had more questions for Jen.

'Will my dad get into trouble for not telling the police where Les is?' I wanted to get this one out of the way before we once again came in range of the officer in his car.

Jen told me she didn't know.

'Will he ever be forgiven? I mean is there an amount of time that you can be escaped for and then everyone says, okay, you've been out for long enough now, we give up on putting you back in jail?'

She picked up a dead branch and began to swish the flies away from her face, occasionally slapping it on her back, glossy black bodies and silvery wings rising and dispersing, only to settle again. 'No,' she finally said.

'I don't believe there is. I guess you have to spend the rest of your life running.'

'That seems so unfair.' I wanted to be on Les's side and Steph's side and her side. 'It's not like he would've been in jail forever.'

She handed me the bag of ingredients and bent down to dislodge a piece of gravel from her sandal. The bag was heavy, but the milk was cool against my skin, and I offered to carry it the rest of the way home for her.

'You have to be quiet now,' she warned me as we came out onto the road where the police car was still parked.

The officer was awake, sitting on the edge of the bonnet and watching us as we walked side by side, neither of us uttering a word.

'Heard from your boyfriend?' His eyes were fixed on Jen, and his face was expressionless.

She stared him down. 'I don't think that's any of your business.'

'When he's on the run, we make it our business.'

I glanced in his direction. His skin was blotched from the heat, his mouth tight and mean. He wiped his forehead and took a pack of cigarettes from his pocket, offering one to her.

She didn't even acknowledge the gesture. 'You have the wrong person.' She raised her chin, staring straight at him, and I admired her terribly. 'As I've told you before, my name is Jen and I know nothing about the person you're looking for.'

He sneered. 'So, they make you all the same over there in sheep country?'

It wasn't even vaguely amusing.

'No,' she replied. 'I believe it's the same as here. Identical twins are — as the name suggests — identical. Everyone else is as unique as you are, Constable.'

I couldn't keep the smirk from my face and so I fixed my eyes on a line of bull ants weaving their way through the red dust to a scattering of rocks near the side of the road. I hoped one of them would bite him on the ankle.

The crunch of his boots on the gravel was harsh, and I could smell him — the perspiration on his nylon shirt, the leather of his holster and a high sweet aftershave. He came one step too close, his boot right near the open toes of her sandals. Jen didn't flinch.

'You tell your sister that if she hears one whisper from that bastard and doesn't tell us' — he lit his cigarette, flicking the dead match into the scrub and blowing the smoke right into her face — 'she'll find herself in jail.' And with those last words he spat on the road, the phlegm sizzling on the bitumen.

Jen put her hand in mine and pulled me after her. I had to walk fast to keep up, the bag of food swinging against my leg. I could hear her muttering as she strode faster, the soles of her sandals slapping on the road, 'Arsehole, bastard, arsehole, bastard …'

'Fucker?' I offered, using one of my mother's favourite terms for my father.

She turned to me and grinned. 'Fucker indeed.' And she shouted the word into the sky, loud enough to enjoy yet not too loud to bring the fucker after us.

That night, my father came home with a woman, introducing her as Thea.

They were outside, the light burning through the matchstick blinds and straight into our eyes as we lay on our camp beds in the lounge room. The glass doors were open to the warm evening and the constant sound of my father's voice as he drank more wine, the bottle clinking against the glass each time he poured. Even if they had been quiet, it would have been hard to sleep, and we tossed and turned in the heat, neither of us wanting to witness our father's attempts at flirtation.

Sitting back in the butterfly chair, he told Thea she was wasted in radio. 'Television is the medium for someone as lovely as you.' And he raised his glass in contemplation of her beauty.

She laughed. 'I'm a secretary.' She lit another cigarette and checked her watch, telling him she was going to have to find her way home soon.

'Let me drive you,' he said, knowing full well she would refuse. He was too drunk.

She told him so.

'Then your only choice is to stay the night. Although the house is somewhat full. In fact, my room is probably the only one where we could squeeze you in.'

This time her laughter was a little higher.

My father suggested opening another bottle.

Next to me, Sass rolled over, the metal springs on the camp bed creaking. In the light, I could see she was trying to drown out his words with the pillow over her head.

'And with the police up on the road, you're probably right, I shouldn't drive.'

Thea's voice was clear across the courtyard. 'They must be very keen to catch him —'

My father interrupted. 'He shot one of theirs. Unforgivable in the police code of honour.'

I didn't hear her response. He probably didn't give her time to make one.

'He's an interesting man.' The hiss of a match cut through the stillness. 'He's ill-educated, a brute in many ways. But he's quick-witted. Knows how to hold your attention with a story, can be charming one minute and then — in the next breath — a bully boy without a clue.

'We're going to get a lot of attention when the shows go to air. Some not so good. The police are going to want to know why we didn't hand him over.'

I could see the glow of her cigarette tip as she listened.

'I'm expecting harassment, possibly even charges — but it's important the public hears the story he has to tell. And it's a classic tale: working class, no education, unemployment. Jail is the inevitable destination for someone like him. We've failed him. As a society, we've failed him.'

From the other side of the courtyard, Jen's light came on. She was sitting on the bed, her silhouette clear.

Thea and my father were too drunk to notice.

'Why are they so convinced he's going to visit his girlfriend?' Thea's words were slurred now. She helped herself to another glass of wine, giggling as she almost knocked the bottle over.

'She's pregnant.' My father's voice carried right through the house. 'Silly trollop got herself knocked up just after he escaped, and rather than getting rid of it, she's gone for the whole romantic teen-pregnancy number.'

The sound of Jen's window opening was the scrape of swollen wood against swollen wood, a shudder as she pushed the frame, her voice ringing out harsh and angry. 'It's my sister you're talking about. And the man she loves.' She slammed the window shut and snapped off her light.

For a second there was silence, and then Thea laughed, nervously. 'Whoops,' she whispered as my father leant over to do what he did best — take full advantage of the awkward moment, offering himself as a co-conspirator, or perhaps a comforter; in any event, a man who was more than ready to deliver a full-bodied red-wine kiss and all that followed.

In the morning, Jen made her tea in silence, taking it back to her room and sliding the door shut behind her. Thea was at the kitchen bench, applying her lipstick and powder, and she grimaced at me in embarrassment.

Wrapped in a towel, the hair on his chest still damp from the shower, my father sang as he put the kettle on and buttered a slice of black bread.

Thea nodded towards Jen's room. 'I think someone may be angry.'

My father took a hearty bite out of the bread, and he reached to tickle me under the chin, but I pulled away. He poured himself a coffee, and kissed Thea with a resounding smack on the cheek. 'Time for work. Although how I will be able to keep my hands off you in the office is beyond me.'

She shooed him away playfully and went back to applying her make-up.

'Jen!' he called out in the hallway.

'What?' Her response was equal in volume, although she didn't open her door.

'Can you tell your sister I will be seeing the man she loves sometime tomorrow. If there's anything she would like me to deliver — loving wishes, kind words, or gifts — I am happy to do so.'

He was intending to be conciliatory. I knew that. I'd heard it often enough with our mother. He would bluster and joke and flirt, then there would be a chink of awareness, a crack that revealed a filament flickering briefly, a softening of the voice — so little, really, but enough to make her open her door.

'You shouldn't have said those things.'

She was much younger, alone in a house with strangers, not in her own country, yet she seemed to have no fear about standing up for herself.

He nodded, voice even lower now. 'Point taken.' He called out again. 'Thea, my dear — it's time we were away. Children! Come and give your father a loving kiss goodbye.'

And then he was gone.

The house was always emptier after he left.

Sitting on the floor of the hallway, rolling a tennis ball against the wall, I listened to the sound of his car going up the driveway and then the silence. It was so quiet that I jumped when the telephone rang — I almost knocked it off the table in my haste to answer, my heart thumping in my chest as I realised who it was, the broad accent a dead giveaway to a boy who'd always been drilled in clear enunciation (one of the few things my mother and father agreed on). People who spoke like that were working class. Or worse still, criminals.

Jen was in the shower, I told him, and Ross (I felt very grown-up using my father's name) had left for the day.

'Who are you?' His voice was wary.

I was Ross's son, I replied, the excitement at speaking to a real criminal almost too much for me. He could trust me, I added, if he had any message he wanted to pass on.

There was silence on the other end of the line.

'I need to speak to Steph.' He sounded worn down. 'Tell her to call me as soon as she can. This is the number —'

'Wait,' I said. I was scrabbling for a pen and paper, reaching across the kitchen bench for a shopping receipt and a pencil. 'Okay,' and I took down the details, repeating them to him as my mother had taught me, only to find that he had hung up before I got to the end.

The plan was simple. Jen would walk over to the Donaldsons' and be Steph for the day. Steph would come here and be Jen.

'And?' I didn't understand.

'She needs you — or at least one of you.'

Sass tore the crusts off the bread, took one bite and pushed it away. 'He always gets this shit.' She told Jen she was in. 'Anything is better than sitting around here killing time.'

Steph wanted to see Les. They had arranged a place to meet. If she took us with her, the police would think it was Jen and wouldn't follow.

I felt I was living an episode of *Matlock*.

'What do we have to do?'

'Just go with her,' Sass said impatiently. 'It's not brain surgery.'

We took a taxi to the closest train station, both Sass and I glancing behind us to see if we were being tailed. The road was empty. Steph stared out the window, silent, apart from monosyllabic replies to the driver's attempts at conversation. It was hot again, and the air that came in was dry and dusty, grit settling on our skin.

We waited while she paid the driver, and then followed her, still silent, down to the platform. There was no one else in our carriage. Sass took a seat on her own, legs stretched out, chin resting in her palm as she watched the slow build of suburban density culminating in the knot of tracks just outside the city.

'Where are we going?' I asked Steph.

She checked the station map and pointed. 'Five more.'

Close to Dullsville, I thought, and I suddenly wished I were home in my room in my mother's house. I was a little scared now, although I would never have admitted it to either of them. I wondered whether Sass felt the same.

At the station, Steph checked the scrap of paper with the address written on it. 'Can one of you ask the guard for directions?'

Sass took it over. I watched her at the ticket window, leaning in, nodding and then returning to us. 'About a ten-minute walk.'

As far as I could tell, no one had followed us. I glanced around. There could be police lurking behind trees, a SWAT team hidden in upper windows, plainclothes detectives spying out of car windows as we passed. Anything was possible. Yet, walking along the footpath past houses closed up to the heat of the day, neatly swept paths and swing sets in front gardens, I felt reassured by the familiarity. This was the land I knew.

'When did you last see him?' I asked Steph, my voice surprisingly loud after our silent journey.

She was startled, and Sass punched me on the arm. 'You're a dickhead.'

'No one heard me,' I hissed.

Steph's face was pinched and drawn, and slightly flushed from the heat. 'I'm sorry,' she said. 'I don't feel very well.' She wiped a slick of sweat from her forehead. 'I think I'm going to be sick.'

As she bent over the dried heads of hydrangeas bordering one of the gardens, she vomited, her back heaving. She turned on the tap at the side of the house and splashed her face, drinking great gulps of water from her cupped palm.

'That's better,' she said.

The place we were headed to was just the same as all the others: respectable, suburban, not where you would expect a man on the run to hide out.

It was Steph who knocked on the back door, a pattern of sharp and slow raps on the timber, her fist clenched. The three of us waited in the sun, blistering hot as it bounced off the white gyprock walls and cracked concrete steps. Sass's face was pale as she squinted, and I saw that she, too, was nervous. She tapped her fingers against her thighs, an agitated rhythm as we waited.

We heard him before we saw him, the sound of his footsteps, and the door opening a crack to reveal an ordinary young man, wide-eyed and frightened, a gap-toothed grin of such relief as he saw Steph.

She didn't move for an instant and then, her sob

guttural, animal, she fell into his hold, all of her body shaking.

'Oh god,' she cried. 'Oh god.' And she stepped back to absorb him, laughing and then crying again as he held her close.

'We haven't got long,' he told her.

'What do you mean?'

'I told Jezz to call them.'

She moved away. 'Who?'

He had his hands on her shoulders now, and I could see his face, the fine line of acne along his jaw, the spasm of a vein in his forearm, his whole body fever-pitched, fine-tuned, tensile and so close to collapse.

'The cops.'

As he uttered the words, she shook her head.

'I can't do it anymore,' he said. 'I can't keep running.'

And she slid down to the ground, her back against the wall, her knees drawn to her chest, reaching out for his ankles to bring him down with her.

We waited, Sass and I, in the shade of the back sunroom, drinking tall glasses of water, the television in the corner on low — an afternoon movie starring Doris Day and Rock Hudson. I guess we both knew they were in the front bedroom having sex, but neither of us said a word, we just watched the show, not laughing at any of the jokes, not even hearing what they were saying.

Outside a dog yapped insistently until it was silenced

by a croaky woman's voice calling out to it — 'Daphne' — the name a quavering tremble, just enough to make it stop for a moment or two, before the barking would commence again. There was also the sound of a sprinkler, ticking back and forth across a nearby lawn, and from somewhere in the distance, the splutter of a mower starting and stopping.

'How are we going to get home?' I asked Sass.

She glanced at me, flicking her eyes straight back to the television screen as she spoke. 'The same way we got here, I guess.'

'But what happens if she goes with him when they take him back to jail?'

Sass shrugged. 'The police will drive us.'

I wanted to call our mum.

'You can't,' Sass said.

'Why?'

'Because we don't know,' she said. 'Maybe we heard it wrong. Maybe he isn't going to hand himself in, maybe it's all going to be okay.' She kept her eyes on the screen.

From out on the street we heard kids playing. It sounded like cricket, the slap of the ball against a plastic bat, followed by a 'Howzat' as someone got out. There was the beep of a horn and shouts, and far, far away a Mr Whippy van, the faint strains of 'Greensleeves' tinkling in the fading afternoon.

'Do you think we'll be here for much longer?'

Sass just shrugged again, but she shifted over on the

cane couch, and I went and sat nearer her.

'We could call Dad,' I suggested.

'As if he'd care.'

The telephone rang in the hall but no one answered it. A clock chimed five, each dong thudding heavy in the carpeted hush of the front room.

And then we heard it, the police siren, distant and then closer, its harshness coming to a stop right outside the house.

The bedroom door opened, followed by the front, letting in a blast of late westerly light, flooding golden through the house.

'He's in here,' Steph said.

The policeman's voice was shotgun loud as he told Les to get down on his knees, hands behind his back. 'Now.' The sound cracked through those rooms, shuddering against the walls as I moved closer to Sass.

'Don't!' Steph screamed. 'He's given himself in.'

We could hear her crying, the slam of the car door again and the sound of another policeman as he told Les to get to his feet. 'You little piece of shit.'

I think they would have hit him if we hadn't come in then. Sass and I stood at the entrance to the lounge room, two children they didn't know were there, and it was Sass who spoke, who told them to stop.

'Don't hurt him,' she said, her voice high and clear. 'You've got him. You don't need to hurt him.'

It was enough to stop them, her words bringing

everything to an instant of stillness as they saw us, brother and sister, hand in hand in the doorway.

'Who are you?'

Sass tried to speak but Steph cut in, crying as she explained that we had nothing to do with any of this.

So we just stood there, ignored while they walked Les down the drive and into the waiting wagon. They probably would have laid into him once they got him in the back. But at least it didn't happen in front of Steph. And I watched as she followed, escorted down to the second car, leaving us there in that house with the youngest of the policemen, his eyes betraying his fear as he tried to be a grown-up.

'Show's over,' he told us, his voice deeper than I had expected, and he looked at Sass and me, two children almost as tall as him, the three of us waiting for someone in charge.

North from South

It was almost dark when they stopped for the van at the side of the dirt road. Jai was the one who noticed it — he was driving, so he had to pay more attention than Kat — and when he pulled over she wasn't even sure why.

He left the driver's door open, and she could hear him talking, his drawl hard to hear above the heavy buzz of descending insects. She thought about leaning over to take a look, but the heat had worn her down, and she stayed where she was, clammy thighs sticking to the torn seat.

They'd been at the waterhole, floating in the tepid green in a bid to cool down. It was Kat's suggestion. Jai had been quite content to continue doing his books, but Kat was bored. The truth was, she'd been bored since she arrived a week ago, the complete enervation only slightly alleviated by their sweaty fucks in the evening, so it wasn't like the boredom of that afternoon was any different or more intense than it had been to date. She just gave it a little more voice.

'Draw me a map,' she'd said, 'and I'll go myself.'

He'd tried, constantly scribbling out his attempts at marking the turnoffs when he realised she had no idea of any of the local landmarks.

'It can't be that hard,' she'd protested. 'I mean, other people find their way around.'

They were out on the verandah, thick palm leaves pressing close, the lurid pink of the bougainvillea harsh in the midday heat, the lawn lush and green as it sloped down towards the other houses in the community, each also circled by dense vegetation.

She could walk to the dam, but she'd done that yesterday and the day before, picking off the leeches after each swim, their swollen bodies drunk with her blood.

She slumped on the cane sofa and sighed.

He shook his head in resignation. He would take her. But not for an hour or so.

She knew how loose his notion of time could be, but it was better than nothing. She would wait, drinking lukewarm tea and smoking his tobacco, her agitation temporarily lulled by the possibility of actually leaving this place. And she listened to the moan of a female singer he liked and the irritatingly slow clatter of his fingers across the keyboard as he typed an email to one of the three women who sold his shirts at the local markets.

Eventually, he stopped, smiling at her as you would a child.

'We'll go,' he told her, and he ruffled her hair until she ducked out of his reach.

Kat had met Jai ten years ago, when she was only fifteen and just out of school. She'd been expelled for telling the science teacher to get fucked. (The truth was a little more complex: he had been sticking his hand up her skirt whenever he crept up behind her at the bench, and she'd tried to slap him off, swearing at him when he failed to get the message. But there'd been no point in trying to explain that to the principal.)

After a few months she'd taken a job at the supermarket, the checkout even more mind-numbing than school had been. One afternoon, when she left work, there was an accident out the front: a car slammed into a dog, the tyres screeching as the driver fled, leaving the animal whimpering in the middle of the hot bitumen. Jai came to help her as she tried to lift the limp and bloody body.

He was dead before they got to the nature strip, the last of his life gone in moments. Crouching in the weeds, stroking the blood-matted ears, Kat cried, aware of how rare this was, her tears strange against the heat of her skin.

They couldn't just leave it there. She turned to Jai, hoping he would be the kind of person who knew what to do in a situation like this.

Lifting the dog once more, he carried it to his ute and laid it carefully on the back tray. Kat went with him without thinking. There was a vet three blocks away, and he drove slowly, trying to distract her with talk, because they could both hear the sound of the dog sliding on the metal, its lifeless body becoming stiff in the sun.

And that was how they became friends. Each time he came to the supermarket, he went to Kat's queue, no matter how long it was. Sometimes he'd wait for her to finish and take her out for a beer. They'd smoke joints in the garden of the pub, while he talked about moving up north, trying communal living, growing his own food, and she would tap her feet, impatient, waiting for him to get the next drink.

In the early days, he tried to have sex with her a couple of times, but she always slithered out of his grasp. Occasionally, she let him kiss her a little longer than she would have liked, but only when she feared there was a danger she had pushed him too far away. Gradually, even that stopped. He was just her friend, a relationship she could never quite understand.

And then he left, moving north, as he'd always wanted, telling her she was welcome to come and visit. Anytime.

It wasn't until some years later that she took him up on his offer. He'd rung her when he came back to Sydney: sometimes she would see him, other times not. It usually depended on how empty her life was. The last time, she'd stood him up. Embroiled in bitter arguments with Vince, she'd had no time for him, and when he called her wondering where she was, she'd lied, pretending her car had broken down, she'd lost his number, jeez she was sorry. Next time, she promised.

A month later, after she and Vince finally split, she got in touch with him. She'd been out late and come home with a man she didn't know. He'd seemed different in the pub. Fun. Someone who drank too much and sang in a sexy, rasping voice, before knocking back another beer and putting his arms around her, the caramel of tobacco on his skin sweet enough to draw her in. He'd started kissing her then and there, pushing her up against the wall and running a hand down between her legs. She'd been in two minds about taking him home, but she'd given in, stumbling through the front door with him and beginning to wish she hadn't as he'd shoved her a little too hard against the stairs, giving her no possibility of asking him to slow down, to let her breathe, and as he'd fucked her, she'd only wanted him to hurry up and finish and leave her alone.

She was good, she'd told Jai, her voice bright when she called him the next morning, the high register on the sharp edge of brittle laughter. Nothing much going down in her life. Just hanging around.

As he listened to her in silence, she could hear the honk of an ibis and the sweet-throated sound of other birds from somewhere out in his garden. He'd told her about the place where he lived, even tried to show her pictures once, and she'd flicked through them, the ash from her cigarette crumbling onto his jeans.

Truth was, the city was getting to her, she said — and she'd had to breathe in to stop the crack in her words. She'd been thinking about taking a trip. Somewhere up north. Maybe coming to see him for a few days?

The pause that followed seemed interminable. But that was Jai. He never spoke fast.

'That'd be good,' he said at last. He'd like to see her.

'Really?' She'd asked the question without thinking, the rush of relief coming out in a torrent of words as she said she wouldn't outstay her welcome, she had a few people she wanted to catch up with, she might even keep going north, try her luck in Queensland, get some work up there and see how she liked it.

'Fine by me,' he said.

On the first evening, they'd drunk beer, smoked a few joints, and she'd soon found herself drowsy. There was a mattress on the floor in a room at the back of the house, and he went to find her some sheets.

She touched his arm. 'Why don't I just … you know?' She leant in closer, unable to say the words, and began to rub her hand along his leg.

He shifted away, surprised.

'You don't want to?'

It wasn't that, he'd explained. She'd never been interested in the past. He'd stopped seeing her in that way.

She hovered between pulling back, offended, and persisting.

Besides, he said, there was someone. She lived on the community. They'd had a thing for a while. She'd ended it. He was still getting over it.

If that was all, Kat said and grinned. What better way to get over someone than a ride on the horse that had thrown you? She'd kissed him, working her hands up his thigh, sensing somewhere inside that she was perhaps too frenzied, her loneliness spinning her furiously across an earth that refused to move, and disliking this but ultimately choosing to ignore it because eventually, she thought, eventually he would have to ruffle.

Which he did. He kissed her deeply as they fucked, moaning so that she, too, felt compelled to moan, and afterwards, as they lay on damp sheets, the fan ticking overhead, he told her he was sorry, he shouldn't have done that. She punched him lightly on the arm.

'Relax,' she said. 'It's just sex.'

After a couple of minutes of waiting in the car, Kat slid over to the driver's side and out onto the road. It was darker than she'd thought. From the beam of the headlights, she could just make out Jai and, next to him, a woman standing against her van, her shape barely discernible — curved, full-breasted — her hair thick and curly. Jai was about to put his arm around her, but she lifted her head and wiped her eyes, suddenly aware of Kat.

There was something in her stance that seemed familiar, and when she said her name — Jackie — Kat stepped a little closer.

'Not Jackie Penfold?' she asked. 'From next door?'

The woman peered out of the darkness, a smile at the corner of her mouth. 'Katrina?' she said. 'Katrina Blake?'

They looked at each other, both stunned. They had grown up on the same street and played with each other until they were about eight. And then Kat and her mother had moved, their few possessions packed and loaded in the car with the usual abrupt speed.

'What are you doing here?' Jackie asked, but she had the van door open now and was rattling the keys in her fingers, as if she wanted to get going.

'Visiting.' Kat put her hand on Jai's arm. 'Catching up.'

He moved away, leaving her holding nothing but the humid air.

Jackie said she had to get home.

Jai was silent when he got in the car. Pissed off, Kat thought, and she was about to make a snipe about how rude Jackie had been, you'd think she'd pretend to be interested in what Kat had been up to, or at least explain why she had to rush off. The words were there, but as she turned to Jai, she didn't utter them.

'You okay?'

He didn't answer, and for once she had the sense to remain silent, touching his hand briefly in an attempt at comfort.

When they got home, he told her he was going for a walk.

The lightning was shattering the glassy evening sky, and the rumble of thunder was close enough to suggest the evening storm wasn't far off. But Jai didn't seem to mind. He liked the rain.

Each night he had cooked for her — vegetable curries, brown rice, lentils — the kind of food Kat hated. But tonight she missed it. She'd never been good at preparing a meal. She thought about heating up the previous evening's leftovers and decided to eat it cold, sitting on the verandah, watching the storm roll in.

Running her finger around the edge of the bowl, she wondered whether she could live here. Be Jai's girl. She considered the idea, the positives and the negatives stacked up like two piles of coloured beads. He'd always been just Jai, willing to buy her a drink, listen to her, there when all other options failed. It was only now, as her life had become even more aimless than usual, that she'd begun to see the value in all he offered — and to sense that she might have missed the boat.

His place was an entire world, and he'd built it himself. When she first arrived, he showed her the outdoor bathhouse, the kitchen curved around a massive tree trunk, the rows of cupboards to store his work, each one a slightly different size, the hand-painted canvas blinds that you could roll out to shelter from the fierce sun. She'd been surprised at how special it was, and she'd told him he should be proud. 'You made all this,' she'd said in wonder.

She put on some music and sat at his desk. Above it was a calendar marked with each of the markets held across the region, who was going to staff the stall, and the likely amount of stock that would be needed.

Kat noticed Jackie's name. She was down for the Channon.

She opened another beer, gulping it greedily as she turned on Jai's computer. She had her feet up, and the scab on her knee had cracked again to reveal a weeping sore. The previous evening Jai had washed it down for her with warm tea-tree oil, and told her to keep it clean. She'd called him a nana, laughing and splashing him with water from the bowl. Don't, he'd scolded as it had almost hit his eyes. She'd flicked another arc in his direction, knocking the bowl over when he put it on the ground.

The computer whirred into life, and she called up his emails, not sure what she was searching for, just bored.

There were messages from people she'd never heard of, most of them relating to his business. All dull. She flicked over to the sent box.

The first one she opened was to Jackie.

Dear Jacks,

I know you have a lot in your life and Rosie isn't easy. I want to be there for you. If you still feel it's all too much and you need some time, I'm not going to go strange. You can do the markets whenever you need to. I'm here.

She scrolled down, opening another one with an attachment, sent about three months earlier.

Missing you. Let's go away like we said we would. Have some time on our own.

In the attached image, Jackie was facing the camera, her dark brown eyes sparkling, her curls escaping out of a scarf, her tanned skin smooth and plump. She was a bit chubby around the arms, but then Jackie always had been large.

Kat examined her reflection in the window. She lifted her top and saw her flat stomach and small breasts. She turned to look at her back, giggling as she did so because it was hard to check out her backside when she'd had three beers and not much to eat. She slapped her rump before turning the music up another notch. She moved closer to the glass, noticing the fine lines across her face. Too much sun. There were circles under her eyes. She'd never been a good sleeper. She was on the brink, she thought. Still a bit of life left, but not a lot.

She had no idea how long Jai had been standing there. He was by the door, half in, half out, his hair wet and his T-shirt sticking to his skin.

'Whatcha doin'?' Kat sidled up to him, swinging her hips as she did so and taking another swig of the beer. 'Wet enough?' She ran her fingers down the slick of his forearm. It was only then that she realised he was staring at the computer, the image of Jackie across the screen.

Putting his head in his hands, he told her he'd had enough.

She thought it was her prying, the fact that the photo was up, and she began to apologise, a flurry of silly excuses that were clearly lies, when she realised he wasn't even listening. He was crying, a deep, dark heaving that so dismayed her she jiggled up and down, up and down, telling him not to do that, please don't do that, until eventually she, too, slid down to the ground and put her arms around him, her whole being as useless as a feather against the weight of his grief, while outside the rain eased and the insects took up their familiar drone.

It was Jackie who told her about Jai's death, five years later. She phoned out of the blue, and it took Kat a few seconds before she put the name and the person together.

Kat was living in Port Macquarie then, working in a pub. She'd been pregnant when she arrived, although she hadn't known that for a couple of months. Her period had never been reliable. And then it seemed as soon as she found out, she lost the baby.

It could have been Jai's. Probably was, in fact. If she'd gone ahead and had it, she didn't know what she would have done about telling him.

She'd left him the morning after he'd gone out walking across the rain-soaked lawns, returning to find her looking through his emails. Later that night, lying next to her in bed, he'd told her that he'd been to Jackie's. He'd wanted to know what was wrong, but Jackie hadn't wanted to see him. When he'd refused to leave, she'd come out into the deluge to tell him what Rosie, her daughter, had accused him of, but she couldn't utter the words. Eventually she said it. Had he tried it on with Rosie? She'd pummelled him over and over on his arms and chest as he remained silent in the rain that pelted down every evening in summer, relentless and wearing.

On her side of the bed, Kat had said nothing.

'I didn't do it,' he told her.

She nodded, without turning to face him.

The next morning she was up early, her bags packed. Time for her to get going, she'd said. You know me, never that good at staying still. Got people to see along the coast.

If he was surprised, he didn't show it. He told her that was fine, not even offering her a lift into town, so that she had to ask him if he could take her.

He'd carried her bags out to the car.

'It'll work out,' she'd said when they parted, unable to say any more than that.

She'd booked the bus to Port Macquarie, certain that she was heading north, until some weeks after she'd begun work in the front bar of the Beach Hotel, only a few metres up from the caravan park on the river. A tourist had left a map behind one night, and as she'd thrown it into the bin, she'd realised her mistake.

'Jeez.' She fished it out of the rubbish.

Mike, the manager, came over and asked if she was okay.

She nodded, and then she admitted to her foolishness, trying to laugh at herself as she confessed.

He'd poured her a drink, grinning as he did so. 'To mistakes,' he'd said, raising a glass to her.

When Jackie told her about Jai's accident, Kat didn't know what to say.

'I couldn't find you in time for the funeral,' Jackie said.

Kat told her it was okay, they'd kind of lost touch.

She was sitting on the balcony, the shops and cafés below her and, beyond them, the sparkling turquoise line of river. The phone was sweaty in her hand. From behind her, she could hear the groan of the plumbing as Mike turned on the shower. His wife was away with the kids this week and he'd been at her place every night.

'You know he left you some money?'

Kat picked at the flaky nail polish on her toenails, not wanting to ask why. She knew she didn't deserve it.

She asked Jackie another question instead. 'So, you two made up?'

There was silence. Mike was singing in the shower now, his voice deep, content, the song of a man who had more than enough. She wanted to tell him to shut up.

'We did.' Jackie chose her words carefully. 'Rosie was difficult. She told stories. I didn't know what to believe; I had to believe her even though I didn't.'

'Did she tell you it was a lie?'

'Kind of.'

'What do you mean?'

'She said enough for me to know. She wanted to hurt me. He wasn't the type to do something like that.'

'Sure.' She knew she sounded like she didn't believe Jackie, but she did. Even at the time of leaving, she'd known, but there had been something in her that had only wanted to run. 'How much did he leave me?' she asked.

'He had a lot,' Jackie said. 'More than anyone expected. He left you sixty.'

Her intake of breath was sharp, a cold hollow whistle of air that slipped into her lungs and silenced her. Enough for a deposit, she thought. Enough to study. Enough to make a change.

She heard Mike getting ready to leave, the coins in his pockets clunking as he pulled on his jeans. He'd wave to her soon, mouth that he would catch her tonight and nod towards the pub, which was only a block away, and then he would close the door behind him, his footsteps echoing on the cement stairs as he made his way down the fire escape, checking that there was no one there to see him.

'Why'd he leave me so much?' The sunlight was hurting her eyes, and Kat stood now, watching Mike cross the road, never once turning back to look at her as he let himself into the dim front bar with its smell of damp carpet, the huge verandah shading it from the clean dazzle of the river and sky and sun beyond.

'I guess he was fond of you,' Jackie said.

Kat turned away. As she slid the glass doors to her flat closed, she caught a glimpse of her reflection. Inside, the bed was unmade, and Mike's coffee cup was where he had left it on the floor, waiting for her to pick it up. She sat down on the mattress and began to cry.

'It's okay,' Jackie said, and Kat knew Jackie thought she was crying for Jai or, more precisely, for having not been there when he needed a friend. But Jackie was wrong. The tears were for herself, and the fact that she didn't even know her north from her south, or a good thing from a bad thing.

I don't deserve it, she was about to say, but instead she asked Jackie what she had to do to collect the money.

That afternoon, as she sat in the park outside the pub, a teenager with two kids crossed the square in front of her, one in a pram, the other trailing behind. Kat watched as the child dropped his packet of chips on the ground, his howl loud. The mother turned and snapped. 'It's your own fault,' she told him. 'You never watch what you're doing.' She slapped the kid on the arse and kept walking.

Mindy, Mike's labrador, slunk over from the hotel, eating the scraps before the seagulls discovered they were there, glancing up guiltily once she'd finished, and then having one last sniff of the pavement to check she hadn't left anything behind.

Sitting in the sun, Kat found herself remembering that first meeting with Jai. She wished she'd asked him to stop the ute as they drove to the vet. It had felt wrong, both of them trapped in the cabin, the dog sliding across the hot metal tray.

She stood slowly, knowing now what she should have done. She should have held it, the bloody heaviness of its lifeless body cradled on her lap, rather than leaving it alone in the heat. But she hadn't. And she pushed the heavy doors that divided the heat of the day from the dark bar, and went in to work.

Mirrored

For three weeks we had been travelling through Rajasthan, eight of us on a mini-bus, together to celebrate an anniversary. I had brought my daughter, Anna, and Jude and Aisla had their son, Miles. Sal, who had just left her girlfriend, had come on her own. She had known Frans and Simon the longest, having once shared a flat with them, years ago. Built on a rooftop perched over the glitter of Bondi, it was the place for parties: nights of drinking, dancing, and falling in and out of love, in a time before we had children and our lives had ossified into families and couples.

It was almost winter, and in Rajasthan the nights were cool, the days warm and dry. This was to be the last stop — Jaipur to bring in the New Year — before travelling north to Delhi, where we would part ways, some of us returning home, some continuing to explore India.

Anna and I were to be the first to leave, and I was ready to go. The relentless crush of life, the noise, clamour, smells and business of living, pressing right up on my skin, had worn me. On the good days, I found it exhilarating; but on the bad, I wanted only to be able to walk along a street, alone.

The bus gave us some respite. We would each take our seats (I would often choose to be by myself), the world separated from us. I could see the dust and the dirt outside, the smear of plastic bags and bottles, the trucks careering down the narrow roads, the camels loaded so high with sticks they looked like giant emus, the motorbikes weaving in and out of the traffic, and the brilliance of the saris on women in stark contrast to the old men in white who sat, cross-legged in the dirt, playing cards. I could hear it all as well, the honking of horns, the roar of engines, a constant noise hovering above the smell — diesel, dust and dung, pungent in the heat. It was a cacophony for all senses.

But this was not the only reason I was ready to head home. At night in the hotels, when Anna was asleep, I would creep out to the roof terrace or garden and turn on my phone. As the screen lit up, I hoped for a message. I had only sent one myself, a couple of brief lines that had taken me an hour to compose. It was two days before I received his reply — *so good to hear from you* — words that promised nothing, and yet I wanted to see them as offering so much more.

His name was Lewis, I told Sal in the bus, careful to keep my voice low, although as Anna was four seats away and the rattle and roar of the engine loud, it was unlikely she would hear.

I felt the heat in my skin as I finally uttered his name, and I bit on my top lip to suppress the embarrassed smile I knew was there.

He was a builder, in charge of the renovations on the house next door.

Sal waited for me to continue.

I had known him years ago, although initially I had no recollection of the boy in the form above me at school. Lewis Longbottom, he said sheepishly, and I'd remembered. It was a name that led to grief when you were growing up — long arse, tall butt, stretch bum — they'd tried every combination and he'd just grinned, sticking his finger up at them all.

I commented on how good his memory was.

'Not really.' His eyes sparkled. 'I had a crush on you.'

'And I haven't changed at all?'

'Not a jot.'

'It's always the way.' I raised my eyebrows. 'No indication of all that life lived showing on the exterior.'

He was tall and lanky, and ready to laugh, his large crooked mouth curled up at the corners.

He was a lazy builder, he said the first morning he came over for coffee. 'I wouldn't hire me,' he warned. 'If you need anything done, that is. It bores me. I like the planning and the end result, but all that stuff in the middle — that's the tedious bit. Hate it.'

'The same could be said for a lot of life,' I said.

'Lucky I've got my crew. They can do the work while I finally get to know you — after all these years.' He winked, his brilliant blue eyes sweet as the spring, and as he bent forward, moving a little closer, his whole body swayed to the slow lilt of music, soft on the radio behind us.

In the bus we lurched to a halt, the driver leaning on his horn. The corner we had to turn was too narrow. In front of us there were tuk-tuks, bikes and cars; beside us, children stared up at the row of white faces in the window above them.

'I think we're going to have to walk,' Frans told us.

He had taken the role of tour guide, with Simon as his assistant. On our first night, in the crowded Delhi hotel dining room, they had told Anna and Miles about when they met in India, two decades earlier. It was the train to Bihar that did Miles in. Eyes wide as he listened, the story became embedded, colouring our entire journey. It also frightened Anna, but at twelve, and three years older than Miles, she was more able to compartmentalise the experience as belonging to Simon and Frans, and not herself.

Simon said that Bihar was the poorest state in India. 'It's beggars and bandits and thieves,' he explained.

'As we approached the border, the guard came to our carriage. He told us we had to get out, now.' Simon pointed at Frans. 'He argued, of course, but not for long.'

Frans rolled his eyes at the children. 'Me? Would I argue?' He was hamming it up for them, his Dutch accent heavy as he protested his innocence.

When they nodded, he swiped at each of them with his napkin.

Simon continued. 'The guard took us to a metal carriage, with no windows or seats, and he told us we had to go in there.'

'And I argued.' Frans rolled his eyes again, grinning at his audience. 'Of course.'

'No, you didn't. Not by then.' Simon went on. 'It was night time and freezing. You know how cold metal gets at night? It was like an ice box. The guard had told us we were not allowed to open the door for anyone, no matter how determined, fierce or pleading they were. We had to stay there, in that carriage, until he came and let us out. We huddled close to each other on the floor all night.'

Frans took up the story. 'And all night, there was banging on the door and on the walls of the carriage, and on the roof. Each time we stopped at a station, the pleading would begin. *Let us in. Let us in.*'

'And did you?' Miles asked.

'No,' Simon told him. 'We kept everything locked.'

'So, who was it?' Anna wanted to know. 'Who was knocking?'

'There were bandits sometimes. Desperate people just wanting to get on the train at other times. It was the scariest night of our lives.'

'And the best.' Frans winked. 'Meant he had to lie nice and close.'

'We're not catching a train, are we?' Miles could not hide his anxiety.

Simon told him no before Frans had a chance to tease him. 'A bus,' he said. And then, seeing he needed further reassurance: 'And we're not going anywhere near Bihar.'

But despite their efforts to comfort him, from the third day Miles wanted to go home. He never said, but we all knew. He didn't want to eat, or leave the hotel or the bus. Aisla was distressed; Jude, cranky. They argued frequently, their voices a murmur from the back seat, while Miles stayed up the front, sitting close to Frans, who tried to tease him out of his misery. And when he couldn't sit with Frans, he sidled next to Anna, who kept her earphones in and a book open, ignoring his attempts at friendship.

Now, as he waited by the side of the bus, he tried to stand close to his father, but Jude just moved away.

Frans told us all it was impossible to drive right up to the hotel. 'We have to get our suitcases,' he said. He took out the whistle we'd given him as a joke and blew into it, the sound shrill. The schoolchildren who had gathered to watch the strange spectacle jumped, and when Frans clapped his hands in mock teacher mode, they giggled.

Tuk-tuk drivers clustered around, wanting to take us or, failing that, our cases. Fifty rupees, forty — the bartering had begun.

'Which hotel?' one asked. When Sal answered, the driver wagged his finger.

'Very, very bad,' he said. 'I know a good hotel. Just around the corner. I take you.' He picked up one of the cases.

Frans seized it from him.

'We have a hotel,' he told him. 'And we're walking.'

'I don't want to walk,' Miles complained.

Aisla put her arm around him and said it wasn't far. Jude told him to snap out of it. Anna gave me a look. I knew Miles irritated her. 'But try to be nice,' I always urged.

She stood there now — her sheet of pale gold hair in a single plait, her eyes deep grey in the light, her skin the smooth olive of her father's — and I was struck, as I often was, by the startling emergence of her beauty. Coupled with her complete lack of awareness of who she was becoming, it was almost too much to bear.

Behind her, one of the tuk-tuk drivers had his eyes fixed on her, and I wanted to tell him she was a child. Instead, I took her hand in mine, relieved she didn't pull away, and unplugged one of her earphones as I kissed her on the cheek.

The hotel was only two minutes away. Our suitcase wheels rattled across potholes and we were followed by children and dogs. One little girl kept tapping on Miles's forearm, wanting to know his name.

'Tell her,' Jude instructed, until Aisla told him to give it a rest.

I avoided Sal's gaze.

Anna wanted to know what it was going to be like.

'I don't know,' Frans replied.

'You haven't stayed here before?'

He hadn't, but he assured her it was going to be special. 'This is the place where we have our party,' he said. 'To celebrate the New Year and to celebrate our love.' He glanced behind him at Simon, who winked at Anna, rolling his eyes as he always did whenever Frans became over-demonstrative.

Behind the wooden gate, a peaceful garden was dotted with white tables. Peacocks picked their way across the grass, the great fans of their tails tucked tight, glittering jewels of colour flashing as they ruffled their feathers and then decided against the brilliance of full display. Behind a bank of trees, you could see the hotel, deep verandahs leading down to the lawn.

All was quiet. No traffic. No people. Nothing.

Sitting out in the late afternoon, drinking cool glasses of Limca and picking at the edge of a paratha, I told Sal the truth about Lewis. We were alone now: Simon and Frans were sorting out the following evening's arrangements, Aisla had taken a tuk-tuk to a shop she wanted to visit, Jude had found a museum, and we had decided to let the children be, leaving them in their room with their Nintendos.

'He's married,' I said, surprised at how ashamed I was at the admission.

She didn't miss a beat. 'Happens to the best of us.'

'What? Marriage? Or falling for a married man?'

'Both if you're unlucky.'

He had told me after we first had sex. 'I should have told you,' he had said. 'I just didn't know how. And I was scared you'd tell me to rack off.'

Which I wouldn't have, but I didn't let him know that. I would have said yes no matter what. I would have risked life and sanity and perhaps, even for an instant, my own child. It had been four years since I had split from Michael and just as long since I'd had sex. When the offerings are that infrequent, who has the strength to say no?

But that wasn't the only reason. When he kissed me, I wanted to breathe in the very air from his lungs. When he smiled, I wanted only to cover his mouth with my own. When he walked up the stairs to my house, his fingers tapping out a rhythm on my front door, I slid down to the floor, helpless and wanting to hold that, just a little longer, before I let him in, all of me alight in his presence.

'An unhappy marriage, I presume?' Sal said.

The truth was, I didn't know. I hadn't asked him. I hadn't wanted to give him the chance to lie to me.

Next to me in bed, while his crew did all the work

next door, he could slide from making promises to gentle disengagement within seconds. He couldn't come next week. There was a new job on the other side of the city. 'But soon,' he assured me. 'I'll get them set up and then I'll be back.'

'When?' I hardly dared ask.

He sang songs to me, confessing he'd once wanted to be a rock star. 'Bass player,' he said. 'I used to form bands with anyone who'd have me. But they'd never have me for long. Not when they found out how few tunes I knew.'

'It's not like I want a relationship,' I told Sal, who was trying to catch the waiter's eye. 'I mean, we could go on like this.'

'And you'd never want any more?' Sal's look was similar to the one I gave to Anna when I knew she was lying, floundering on the tip of an untruth. 'You're not the first.' She was trying to be kind.

I narrowed my eyes. 'The first what?'

'The first to speak such total crap.' She signalled the waiter, letting him know we wanted the bill, and reached across to take my hand. 'I'm sorry,' she said. 'I didn't mean to be so blunt. And I don't judge you, or him, or anyone for that matter. But just don't lie to yourself. See it for what it is and you'll suffer a lot less.'

I had almost not come to India, scared that if I left him, he would disappear, severing the few threads that held us together. The bombing in Mumbai would have made it easy. Watching news reports of the chaos and terror, I had seized upon the excuse, telling Frans and Simon I couldn't take Anna there now. They had urged me to think about it and I had promised them I would. But it wasn't the slow gathering of reason that made me change my mind.

I saw him. It was early on a Saturday evening, the warmth of the day still lingering in the empty suburban street near the local pool. I had gone to do laps, not bothering to change afterwards, walking to my car in my swimmers, a towel wrapped around my waist, my skin dry and scaly from the chlorine. I only stepped back because I didn't want him to see me like that. He was coming out of a house, standing at the front door as he said goodbye to someone. A friend, I presumed, knowing he did not live around here. And then he kissed her, whoever she was, gently, delicately, in the way he had first kissed me, a question that I was so quick to respond to.

Unable to move, I stayed and watched, clutching my towel tight around myself because I thought that if I let go I might find myself gone, cold air where flesh had once been.

Seconds later, he went back inside, the door closing shut behind them both.

Had it been him? I tried to convince myself I had made a mistake, and I probably would have succeeded if I hadn't seen his car, parked four doors up, an old red Volvo station wagon with a numberplate I was ashamed to admit I had memorised.

I didn't tell Sal any of this. If she thought I was a fool already, there would be no saving me from her scathing assessment should she hear that last bit, the addendum I had failed to reveal.

It was not what I thought, he said, four days before our departure.

Her name was Cally. They had been lovers before he met me. He had told her it couldn't continue some time ago. They were just friends now, but she still wanted more. And so she had kissed him, wanting him to come back inside.

'Which you did?'

Yes, he said. He did. But not to sleep with her. Simply to calm her down.

'How many lovers do you have?' I asked, incredulous.

'Only you,' he swore.

'And your wife.'

He stared at the ground.

'Trust me.'

I wished I could.

Jaipur, Frans had told us, was famous for its Amber Fort.

'Every city is famous for its fort,' Anna had said.

Sensing a possibility to stay in the safety of the hotel, Miles had been quick to join in. 'We don't want to see another fort. It's been a fort a day.'

'Well, I hope it's been more than just one thought a day.' Simon was always quick with the joke. Dad jokes,

Frans called them. You should have been a dad, he would say. And he should have. We all knew that, and they had hoped for it once, trying with various women, including Sal, but always with no success.

The bus drivers were waiting for us in the laneway. The immaculate press of their clothes and the perfect slick of their hair gave no indication that they had eaten by the side of the vehicle and slept inside.

We took our seats, each of us choosing a window and to be on our own.

Looking out, I watched the endless rush of traffic and people while behind me Anna listened to her iPod, also gazing at the street. I wondered what she would make of this trip, how she would frame it on her return, and I turned to talk to her, but she kept her eyes averted.

As we pulled over into the carpark, Simon told us there were two ways up: elephant or foot.

'Are you sure you'll be alright?' I asked Anna, knowing her tendency to pretend she felt no fear. I had seen it in her eyes as she watched the first of the huge leathery beasts lurch up from its knees, the passengers on top swaying against the deep blue sky.

She brushed me aside. 'Of course. I'm not like you. I'm not scared of heights.'

Sal and I took what we thought was the footpath, only to discover halfway up that we had chosen wrongly: the wide stone roadway was used by the elephants and there was little room to squash ourselves against the walls as they lumbered up the hill, the hairs on their hide right up near us as they moved to avoid those coming down.

'Jesus.' Sal jumped back, only just missing a stream of sweet grassy shit. 'We've got to get out of here.'

That morning, before the others had arrived for breakfast, she had apologised for being so harsh.

Embarrassed by my own stupidity, I had told her it was fine. But as I laid out each of my pills (anti-malaria, Travelan and another probiotic), I had wanted to correct her. It had bothered me all night.

'I'm not lying to myself,' I said. 'I do see it for what it is. But you're wrong. It's not going to make me suffer less in the long run.'

She listened. 'You're probably right.'

Now, as we tried to cut across the road towards the stairs that would take us out of the path of the oncoming elephants, we spoke no further about my confession.

'There they are.' Anna's hair gleamed in the winter light, her two plaits hanging down the back of her T-shirt. She and Simon and Frans were on the first elephant, the others right behind them.

'Was it fun?' I asked as we were reunited in the huge entrance, the red sandstone already warm in the morning sun.

It was, she told me, her eyes alight like a child's again, alive from the pleasure of having made it, despite her fears.

Around us, a group of men had begun to gather,

wanting to be our guides. We were used to this now, ignoring them as they waved laminated cards in our faces, offering very good tours, very good indeed.

'See, sir, I am accredited.'

'I have special government pass.'

'No need for audio. No, sir.'

Frans once again took charge. Did we want someone to show us round? Jude always liked a guide, Aisla didn't mind, the rest of us said we would prefer to take this last tour on our own.

It was a public holiday and, despite the early hour, the fort was crowded. Most of the visitors were Indian, a large number of this season's foreigners having been scared off by the terrorist attacks. Crushing through each of the gateways, they paused to take photos, group shots, family shots, portraits; digital cameras glinting as they captured aunties and sisters in saris, daughters dressed in the latest Western gear — tight little shorts, gladiator sandals and T-shirts with nonsensical slogans — and husbands proud in casual sportswear.

Aisla was the first to peel off. She, too, was photographing furiously, intent on patterns and colours for use in her fabrics when she returned, using her charm shamelessly as she asked people to pose for her, giggling with them as they laughed at the mad Western woman interested in taking their image.

Miles joined Jude, Frans and Sal as they headed down to the Sila Devi temple. 'They sacrificed goats here,'

Jude read from his book. 'One every single day, from the beginning of the sixteenth century until 1980.'

'So how many altogether then?' Miles asked.

'Let's work it out.' Jude liked doing that. Working it out. During the brief period in which we were together, more than fifteen years ago, I had told him it simply couldn't be done. 'Us,' I had said.

'But we can work it out,' he had replied, as though we were a problem that had to have a solution.

Two years later, he had met Aisla, who had at first been self-conscious around me. Now, with a child and a house together and all that life between them, we were all simply friends. I rarely remembered the time I spent with Jude, but when I found myself right back there, I wanted only to flee.

As he descended the stairs, telling Miles how to work out the equation, Anna, Simon and I began to wander.

I was, by then, like the children, tired of forts and I walked around, aware of the magnificence of all I saw but unsure how to receive it. I had not read my guidebook the night before, and I dipped in and out of listening to Simon explain what he knew to Anna.

High at the top, you could see the lake, framed by the chalky pink of the walls, and we paused there for some time, none of us speaking as we looked out across the water and the desert beyond. Behind us, passages led in and out of different rooms, sometimes narrow, sometimes wide, the size of the palace so large that it was possible to find yourself alone for an instant, only to be startled by the flap of a bird's wings.

It was an hour or so before we all met up again, quite by accident, but also with a certain inevitability. There were, after all, only so many passages to take. And so we found one another sitting, obvious among all the Indian families, dazzled by the silver and mirrors in a hall that offered a thousand visions from all angles, each one glittering and true.

It was Jude who told me to look at the marble panels. I did not leave Anna for long, less than a minute, just to wander around the closest of the intricate carvings. I could see her the whole time, and I kept watch, returning when the man sat next to her. Overweight and sweaty, he leant in close, wanting his photo taken with the Western girl.

It was just a flicker of doubt — or perhaps anxiety was a better word — but I quashed it, telling myself it was harmless. After all, hadn't Aisla wandered around taking photos of them, wanting to capture the strange exoticism of the mix of Western and Indian, the clash of colour and culture?

Sitting on the other side of Anna to let her know I was there, I squeezed her hand. Opposite us, the man's friends had gathered in a group, all male, all laughing at the sight of him pressed close, mouth wide open in a leering grin.

It would be over in a minute.

One took the photo.

'Another,' the man said, and I felt Anna inching towards me, wanting to get away from him.

It was enough, but stupidly, I didn't speak.

He put his arm around her, so close that his hand touched my shoulder on her other side, and I could smell his skin.

One of his friends started making kissing noises.

Another photo was taken.

He held her tighter, pulling Anna's mouth towards his, and I felt her struggle to push him away, as I also pulled, standing up, to give her the room to move.

'Enough,' I shouted at him.

Simon, who was right behind me, also shouted: 'Let her go.'

Laughing, the man ignored him, reaching for Anna again, but I had her now, and I held her, dragging her away from him and his friends, a row of men surrounding us, ugly grins across their faces.

Later, when we had finally left the fort, and had returned to the hotel, I tried to talk to her.

My attempts after the incident had gone wrong. I had veered between trying to comfort her, venting my own anger, and shouting at Jude.

'It was just a misunderstanding,' he had said, wanting to calm me down.

'A cultural thing?' I had glared at him.

He shrugged. 'I guess so.'

'What?' I stepped closer. 'So, by analogy, every time a man treats a woman like shit, every time there is sexual harassment, gang rape, whatever, it's just a cultural thing?' I had clenched my hands, fingers in my palms, my rage red-hot in the marbled hall, sharp as the hundreds of tiny mirrors around us. I would have slapped him. And then, as I heard Anna still crying behind me, I knew I had to let it go.

Back in our hotel room, I wished that Michael and I were still together and that he was here now. I wanted her to feel the world was safe. Overhead, the fans ticked round and round. In the gardens, they were setting up for our New Year's Eve gathering, laying a special table for us, white cloth, glasses, silverware. We would eat and make a toast to Frans and Simon and their twenty years, and we would begin to reminisce about this trip even though it was not yet over.

I took the headphones out of Anna's ears and told her I wanted to talk to her.

'What he did was wrong.'

She kept her eyes on her knees.

'And you shouldn't feel ashamed. He should be ashamed. And you should be angry.'

Her glance in my direction was furtive.

'You know,' I said, taking her hand in mine, 'the worst thing is that I knew the situation wasn't right.'

'Me, too.' It was the first words she had spoken about the incident.

'From the minute he sat next to you. But I thought that if you just played it nice and let him have his photo, it would be over and done with.'

Her voice was soft. 'So did I.'

'I'm sorry,' I said. 'I should have intervened.'

Sitting on the edge of her bed, I wanted her to look at me.

'You have to trust it,' I told her. 'It's called intuition, truth, inner sense, whatever — but if it's telling you something, don't ignore it. Because there are going to be difficult times in life, hard times, scary times, and you need to listen to that sense. Get away if it's telling you to get away — don't stay there being nice in the hope that everything will be okay.'

Too many words. She reached for her headphones, but I put my hand on hers.

'It's important,' I said, and she rolled her eyes.

I had to let her go.

From the balcony of our room, I could see the garden, darkening in the oncoming night. It was New Year's Eve, I told myself, the start of another year. I would be home in a couple of days, back in the city where Lewis lived, and was, no doubt, celebrating now, kissing someone, his wife or his lover, with a languorous pleasure that had turned me inside out.

As I drew the curtains to our room and told Anna we had to get ready, we were late, she turned on the television, wanting to see the New Year's celebrations from around the world. With the volume down, I, too, watched until the cameras showed us fireworks lit up across the Sydney Harbour Bridge, midnight already there, and as the colours sparkled across that faraway sky, I heard the ping of my phone.

He had sent me a message. I paused, hoping for the strength to ignore it.

He was only ever going to make me sad. I had known that for quite a while now. Yet sometimes the knowledge was just not enough, or perhaps it was, in itself, just too limited. Maybe the intensity of the longing and the excitement and the desire were what mattered, and this was what I should be looking at, my gaze fixed there and not at the end.

And so I reached across the bedside table, telling Anna not to wait for me but to go down to the garden, where the others were no doubt already gathered, old friends wanting to toast a love that had lasted and a year to come.

I would join them soon.

Murramarang

'I've been composing a letter to Margaret in my head,' Eloise said. She had paused, each foot balanced on a boulder, shading her eyes with her hands as she wondered what was the best path forward. Out at sea, a cormorant plunged beneath the surface and re-emerged with its feathers ruffled. 'Every time I come on this walk, I find myself thinking about what I want to say to her.'

The slabs of black rock had broken into smooth pebbles, and those that had been submerged when the tide was high were slippery, a fine pelt of moss covering their perfectly rounded curves. Eloise was heavy-footed and had little balance. When she was in her teens and felt she had to keep up, she would find herself anxious on walks such as this one; now she just took her time, sometimes half sitting as she made her way around to the bay opposite Brush Island, not liking how ridiculous she must appear but not caring enough to pretend she was capable.

Taking Hamish's hand, she stepped down from the last boulder, her feet sinking into the wet sand.

'So,' Hamish asked, 'what would you say to her?'

She was surprised he wanted to know. She'd talked so often about Margaret, and he usually did little to hide his lack of interest in the topic.

'It's not so strange,' she said, 'that I'm thinking about her all the time. Being here reminds me of her — even more so than usual.' She let go of his hand as they continued to walk along the edge of the ocean, picking their way between clumps of glistening black weed washed up with the previous evening's tide.

This was their first holiday at this beach without Margaret and Justin. They had been coming here since Lila turned one, hiring the same house together, while Holly and Andrew, and their three boys, took the house next door. Eight years later, they only had one house. She and Hamish slept upstairs, while Holly stayed downstairs with the kids. Holly and Andrew had separated, and Eloise and Margaret no longer spoke. They had never actively made this decision; rather, Eloise had stopped ringing Margaret, wanting to see whether Margaret would ring her, which she never did. Sometimes she wondered whether it had been the other way round: Margaret had stopped calling her, to see whether she would telephone. Which she hadn't.

She had asked Hamish for his views on this several times, and he never answered, probably because it didn't actually matter. She knew that the undoing had happened last summer, and when she came on this walk, she found herself picking over it, aware of the tender spots and uncovering them carefully.

When she tried to talk to Holly about it, Holly would tell her to let it go. Her tanned legs sticking out of the shade of the umbrella as she kept one eye on her boys, the other on her book, she would say it was just the way it was. 'Go with Hamish and have a walk,' she would urge, despite Eloise protesting that it was too much to leave her with all the kids.

But this morning she'd given in, knowing they'd had little time alone.

'There's a lot I want to say,' she told Hamish as they rounded the headland to where the rocks were flat enough for Eloise to feel safe, so much so that she strode a little faster than she would have liked, in an attempt to make up for how clumsy she had been earlier.

She stopped at the grassy track above the rock ledge. Hamish was just behind her, staring at the waves.

'It's a good swell,' he said. 'Might get the board and head down to Racecourse when we get back.'

He hadn't been listening.

'I miss her,' she said, and she was surprised at the sadness in her voice.

'People go.' Hamish stepped up onto the track and

turned her to face him, both hands on her shoulders. 'You've got to let it happen.'

Holly was the one who first brought them all here. She had come to this beach when she was at school, and she knew it well. In the years when she came with Andrew, she woke Eloise early each morning and together they walked along the windswept stretch of Murramarang, over the grassy headland and down to Bull Pup, a small bay that was calm and clear.

The previous year, when Margaret was still with them, Holly had to take the house next door on her own. She had those two weeks with the kids; Andrew had the next.

'It's all good,' she insisted when Eloise offered any form of sympathy, deftly deflecting any attempts to discuss the fall-out.

Eloise wished that Margaret and Justin had gone next door and that Holly had stayed with them. Margaret had been in a bad mood from the first day, spending hours in her room with the door shut. When she did come out, she sat in the corner, staring out the window at the stretch of beach, giving monosyllabic answers to questions directed at her. She was premenstrual, she said, when Eloise cautiously asked her what was wrong.

On the third night she threw a dish at Justin. 'Why am I doing the fucking dishes again?' she shouted as the china smashed on the ground.

'Because you can't let them sit there for two minutes unwashed.'

Margaret slammed the door behind her, leaving the rest of them under the glare of the kitchen light.

'What was that?' Lila asked, opening the door to her bedroom, her eyes round with the possibility of a drama unfolding.

'It was nothing,' Eloise told her, and Hamish picked her up, turning her upside down as she giggled.

'Should I go after her?' Eloise asked Justin. He was still sitting in the armchair, the shards of china scattered around his feet.

'If you feel the need to give that kind of behaviour attention, be my guest,' and he shrugged his shoulders. Then he sighed.

'What's going on?' Eloise felt guilty. Margaret was her friend, and she should be asking her, but Margaret's mood had been pissing her off. She and Hamish had whispered about it at night, Eloise tentative: Margaret was always tense, difficult to be around; God knows how Justin had put up with her for all these years; and then, ashamed, Eloise would backtrack. Justin's passiveness would send anyone into a fury and there was also the whole child issue: Margaret had always wanted a kid; Justin had always refused.

Justin kicked the pieces of china into a pile. 'She's just being Margaret. She hates her new job, she's sick of our house being unrenovated, she wants to move. Who knows? It could be anything.' He rolled his eyes and turned to the door. 'I'll go and get her.'

Margaret worked in corporate communications for a large finance firm. Her days were long, and she always had her mobile with her, taking quick calls on the balcony at all hours. Justin was a gardener.

'I wish he'd get a bloody job,' she said sometimes, 'instead of relying on me to take care of everything.'

He did have a job, Eloise would venture. Justin's work was sporadic, but when it came in, he earned enough to cover his half of the expenses.

Margaret laughed. 'Fuck. It's not like he can keep doing that forever.'

Each morning Margaret ran. She ran for miles, coming back slick with sweat, her breathing heavy, her shorts and singlet in a crumpled heap outside the bathroom door as she showered. Pinching the roll of flesh above the waistband of Justin's shorts, she would take a nectarine from the bowl on the table and then eat it slowly. That was her breakfast, sometimes her lunch as well.

Hamish cooked scrambled eggs for everyone else, including Holly and the boys. Eloise would always think about saying no because she hated how overweight she was becoming, but then she would smell them and tell him that she'd like a half serve, with just one piece of toast.

Sometimes when she washed the dishes, he would put his arms around her waist, burying his mouth in her hair.

'Reckon we could sneak off?' he asked one morning.

Outside the kitchen window, she could see Holly kicking the soccer ball to Lila, trying to keep it away from her three sons. 'Not now,' she told him.

Lila kicked the ball hard and held up both arms in a victory salute.

'Holly's on her own,' Eloise said. 'And Margaret and Justin are fighting.'

'So?'

He was already tanned from a few days on the beach and he smelt salty and warm. As he kissed her again, she poked him in the ribs. 'Go and play soccer with Holly,' she said. 'She shouldn't have to take care of Lila as well.'

'What's with Margaret?' Holly asked later that day, when the two of them sat under the umbrella.

Eloise tried to explain, but she soon found the excuses she was making on her friend's behalf dwindling, feeble. 'If she hates her work as much as she says, she should leave. It's not like she doesn't have money. And if Justin is making her so miserable, she should leave him, too.' She wiped the sand off her hands and stood to join the children in the water.

Holly looked up at her. And then she said something that surprised Eloise. 'You know, I sometimes wondered whether Margaret had a thing for Andrew.'

'Really?' The thought had never occurred to Eloise. Andrew and Margaret had seemed to enjoy each other's company, but then Andrew was always charming and flirtatious with women. Too much so. He'd had, unbeknownst to any of them, several affairs during his ten years with Holly. But surely not Margaret? 'She would never have done anything.' Eloise realised her response sounded hesitant.

Holly just shrugged.

'She's your friend,' Eloise said.

'Friends don't always behave like friends.'

The sand was burning the soles of Eloise's feet, and she shifted from left to right, waiting as Holly also stood to go for a swim. At the water's edge, Lila jumped in and out of the waves, while Holly's two younger boys dug a hole in the wet sand.

'Last one in is a rotten egg,' Holly called out to them as she raced down to the ocean, leaping over the castle they had built, her body showing no sign of having given birth to three children.

'Just luck,' Holly had said when Margaret had once asked her how she stayed so thin without ever exercising.

That night they had played cards.

Holly had brought the boys over and put them to bed on the floor of Lila's room using cushions from the couch. A southerly had blown in, and the windows rattled, straining on their catches. Eloise washed the dishes this time: while she finished the last of the pots, Margaret dealt.

'Gin rummy,' she said, with only Hamish daring to protest that he found the game boring.

Justin held up the joint he had rolled, checking its perfect shape with some pride, before passing it to Holly to light. She passed it on to Margaret, who also declined, glaring at Justin as she did so. 'As if you need to get any slower.'

'It's a holiday,' Eloise said, regretting it as soon as she did so.

Eloise played two rounds of cards and then said she'd had enough.

'Canasta?' Hamish suggested, now that there were only four of them at the table.

They paired up, and Eloise sat on the couch, flicking through the magazines that had been left by previous tenants. Bored, she picked up Hamish's camera and scanned through all the pictures he had taken. It was a shock to see herself. She looked older than she imagined, with the body of a middle-aged woman, a sunburnt nose and a toothy smile. There was one that particularly appalled her: she was struggling to put up the beach umbrella, her sarong flapping in the wind, making her even larger, her hat an old piece of cloth — while standing to her right were Margaret and Holly, tall, slim and strong. She glanced up at Hamish, who was focused on his cards, and then pushed the delete button. Scrolling through the rest, she began to delete every image that had her in it, even those where she was in the background.

'What are you doing?' Hamish asked.

'Nothing,' Eloise lied.

'Come and sit with us.' His eyes were glazed from the joint.

Later, in bed, he wanted to have sex, and she pushed him away.

'They'll hear us,' she said, pointing in the direction of the room where Margaret and Justin were sleeping.

He turned to her in the darkness. 'What's brought this on?'

She couldn't even attempt to explain. 'I'm just not in the mood,' she told him, her voice crosser than she had intended.

He took his arm away from her, leaving her cold, as he moved away and went to sleep.

Margaret was at the back door, putting on her running shoes, when Eloise came out the next morning. The southerly had passed, and the day was washed clean, new and fragile.

'Want to go for a walk instead?'

Margaret seemed surprised, her expression almost gentle, as she stopped tying her laces. 'You look like Lila.' She smiled, and then stood and stretched, one leg lunging forward, the other behind her. 'Why don't I meet you at Bull Pup, and we can walk back together around the rocks?'

Opening the flyscreen at the back of Holly's house, Eloise called out. 'Come for a walk? The boys are still asleep at our place.'

Holly was already in her swimmers. She put on a shirt and took her oldest son's cap from where it lay on the floor.

The tide was out, with only a slight swell rolling into the broad sweep of hard wet sand. They walked briskly, the sky above still pale. Eloise laughed a little about Lila being in love with Josh, Holly's oldest boy. She had found them top-and-tailing on the mattress on the floor, legs entwined, their faces calm in the deep sleep of childhood. It was good for him to be friends with a girl, Holly said. He had always been so dismissive of them in the past.

As they neared the end of the beach, they dropped their towels on the sand and went into the sea. The tides had been cold that summer, the water like ice, an aching grip on each limb. This morning, however, it was warmer. Eloise swam out, floating on her back as the roll of the ocean lifted her and then let her fall. She was going to be designing a block of apartments when she returned to the city, and she found herself thinking about it each time she was alone (which wasn't often), her thoughts trying to wrap around her approach. She played with the possibility of something more organic, less linear than she had originally considered, visualising the site to see whether it would work. The idea was exciting, and as she swam in, she considered going straight back to the house to take some notes. But then she remembered her promise to herself that she would exercise more often; besides, all the kids would be up now and there would be no solitude.

Drying herself with her towel, she told Holly she was almost looking forward to getting back to work. 'I guess it hasn't been that pleasant here this year,' she added.

'With Margaret?'

Eloise nodded.

The path over the headland was sandy at first. As they climbed higher, it became matted with straw grass, the sharp twigs buried beneath the surface forcing them to put their shoes back on. As they emerged from a dense clump of casuarinas, the kangaroos that were grazing glanced up, on watch as they passed.

'What made you think she and Andrew liked each other?'

Holly considered this. 'It was when we separated. Margaret was so keen to know all the details. And when I told her about his affairs, she was incensed.'

Eloise still found it hard to believe.

'There was something in her manner,' Holly said. 'She's so unhappy with Justin. She's so unhappy with everything. I guess that's when you're likely to sleep with your friend's partner.'

'Maybe she did sleep with Andrew.' Eloise knew her words were a betrayal, but she was angry with Margaret, and so she uttered them, not liking herself for voicing something she knew was probably untrue. 'I listen to her going on about how much she hates work and how unhappy she is with Justin, and most of the time I'm too scared to do anything other than let her speak. And then

I feel like I'm colluding.' It was the most disloyal she had been. 'There is so much that is likeable about her,' she rushed to add. 'Or there was. You know, she can be so biting and funny and lively ...'

Holly seized her arm, just above the wrist, and she stopped, panicked for a second that she was about to tread on a snake.

'What?' she asked, and she turned just slightly to the left and saw Margaret, sitting on the rocks at the bottom of the track, only a few metres away, but surely too far off to have heard what they were saying? Eloise raised her arm in greeting, feeling a flush of colour on her cheeks.

Margaret didn't move. With her eyes on Eloise, she stayed perfectly still, and then she stood and began to walk down the beach.

'Wait,' Eloise called out, knowing she had no chance of catching up unless Margaret chose to slow down. 'Please.'

At the edge of the rocky outcrop that separated Bull Pup from the next bay, Margaret turned.

'Why are you just walking off?' Eloise knew it was a cowardly question.

Margaret's face was pale.

'I didn't mean it,' Eloise said, feeling ill as she recalled her conversation with Holly, unsure as to what Margaret would have overheard.

'It's easy for you,' Margaret eventually said. 'You have work you love and you have Lila.' Bending down to pick up a stick, Margaret's voice trailed off. 'I won't have a kid.'

They had been friends since high school. In all those years, Margaret had been the one everyone liked: she was funny and attractive, she was bright, and Eloise had always felt privileged to have Margaret as a friend. Now, Eloise found herself wishing that their world hadn't spun as it had, that it was still Margaret who was blessed, and her standing in the shadow. That would be easier, she thought in a sudden rush of guilt. That was what she wanted to apologise for, but how could you do that? Instead they had both promised they would each try harder to make the friendship work, and there on the rocks, she had wanted to believe it was possible. Then, looking behind her, Eloise saw that Holly had gone. She must have walked back over the headland, leaving the two of them alone. It was only much later that Eloise wondered at how neatly she had extricated herself.

Back at the house, Margaret showered and went into the bedroom where Justin was still asleep. The kids were over at Holly's and Hamish had gone for a swim. Eloise sat on the verandah and closed her eyes.

Once, years earlier, when Hamish had told Eloise he was not sure if he loved her enough to have children, she had gone to Margaret's house in the middle of the night and knocked on the door until she opened it. Eloise had cried with complete abandonment, unable to stop the tears and explain why she was there.

'He doesn't love me,' she managed.

Margaret said nothing, just took Eloise's arm and led her inside, and laid her down on the other side of her bed, holding her around the waist, trying to soothe her with the warmth of her body.

'It's just what men say,' Margaret told her. 'It's his last fight from the corner, but he loves you. He'll have a kid with you.'

Eloise eventually slept, with Margaret curled close, one arm flung across her stomach, her breath warm and even on her neck. This is what it would be like to be lovers with Margaret, Eloise thought, as sleep began to cloak her consciousness. And she wondered at all the men who had been with Margaret and left her, choosing to turn their back on the sweetness of this place.

Eloise never wrote to Margaret. She composed numerous letters in her head, and she occasionally picked up her phone and brought up her contact details — once, she even drove down her street only to turn around. And then, six months after that last holiday, the one in which there had been just her, Hamish and Holly in the one house, Hamish had told her he was leaving, and she had thought she would die. He was in love with Holly, he said, and although she could see that he, too, was pained, she didn't care. When, she wanted to know. Why?

She wanted only to hurt him as much as he hurt her, because she would wake in the middle of the night and remember coming back from the beach to find them both sitting on the verandah, or perhaps it was just Holly she saw, running down into the ocean, kicking the soccer ball with the boys, eating the food that Hamish cooked, telling them all that splitting up with Andrew had been the best thing that could have happened to her; and Eloise would call Hamish then, abusing him in the middle of the night, crying and begging him to tell her it had all been a terrible mistake.

But the intensity ultimately passed, leaving her with regret for all she had failed to see, and it was not just Hamish and Holly she didn't notice. She found a photograph from the holidays they all used to have together, one of the few she had not deleted. She stood in between them both, Margaret and Holly on either side of her. She remembered how inadequate she always felt, yet as she saw herself there in that image, she liked the wide smile, the light in her eyes, the freckles on her nose, and she could tell how happy she once was. She just wished she'd known it at the time.

Her Boredom Trick

When Clara finally arrives, not only is she late, but she also has her dog with her. Sinead watches as it leaps from the car, Clara letting go of the lead because she needs the little strength she has in her arms to get herself out of the driver's seat, her scarves catching in the door as she shuts it behind her.

'Fuck it,' Sinead mutters, her mother infuriating her already. 'I told her not to bring that animal.'

The dog bounds up the stairs, and Sinead steps in front of her daughter, Zoe, before it tries to mount her, something Zoe hates — even more so now she has some notion of what sex is, thanks to the older boys in her composite grade 3/4 class.

'Down,' Sinead orders, but it's useless. 'We can't take her.' She glares at Clara, who is gathering Zoe in the folds of her loose-fitting kimono jacket, and kissing her on the top of her head. 'You know she has nits,' Sinead adds, but Clara continues to kiss her granddaughter.

'I don't have nits,' Zoe says. 'You combed them out last night.'

'Lice?' Clara, oblivious to Zoe's attempts to squirm out of her hold, kisses her again. 'I'm sure they'll give me just the protein I need.' She turns to Sinead. 'Shall we go?'

First, there is the matter of the dog. It pants, next to them. They cannot take her. Sinead's voice is terse. 'We're looking at houses. The real estate agents won't want her inside.'

'Well, I'll tie her up outside,' Clara replies.

'I don't want her in the car.'

She'll be fine, Clara promises. Besides, if she has to take her all the way back, they'll be so late it won't be worth going. 'And I know you don't want me leaving her at your house.'

'Come on,' Zoe urges, fed up with waiting.

'On one condition.' Sinead has her arms folded across her chest. 'You pay for my car to be cleaned, if she's sick.'

'Of course I would, darling.' Clara has already opened the back door and let the dog jump in on top of Zoe. 'You know you don't even need to ask.'

It's only an hour's drive to Bundeena, but Clara's late arrival means they have to ring the agent and let them know they won't be on time. Clara sees no need. 'It's their job to wait for us,' she says as she opens her window wide to the dust and grit of the road. Sinead insists, and Clara eventually takes the mobile phone and makes the call.

'They'll be there all afternoon,' she says as she hangs up. Pulling the sun visor down, she checks her lipstick, rubbing at where it has bled into the corners of her mouth. 'What a glorious day. How many houses did you ask them to show us?'

There are only four available for rent, and only one that appears to be suitable. The others are either too expensive or too run down, Sinead explains. Clara nods, flipping up the visor, then takes a scrap of paper out of her bag.

'There's a couple for sale as well.' There are addresses scribbled across the crumpled page, torn from one of her many notebooks.

Sinead sighs. It's only talk; Clara has no intention of buying. Sinead's plan is a realistic one. They will rent a place together, somewhere cheap that they can take it in turns to use. They could even get other people in on the lease as well, making it more affordable for everyone.

'So long as it's only one other person,' Clara says. 'I'd like to know I could have decent stretches of time down there if I need it.'

When Sinead protests about the cost, Clara is no longer interested. She smooths out her scrap of paper. 'We'll just see the ones for sale then.'

'Why?' Sinead says. 'You've seen them before. You're not serious about buying one of them.'

'You never know.'

'The agents must hate you.'

'It's not their job to hate me,' Clara says. 'It's their job to like me.' She turns to wink at Zoe, who is quiet.

Sinead glances in the rear-vision mirror. Her daughter has her cheek to the window, her eyes fixed on the blur of trees, houses and cars, rushing past in a stream of colour. Beside her, the dog is sitting up, panting.

'Are you alright, darling?'

Zoe remains silent.

'Are you doing your boredom trick?'

Zoe doesn't answer.

Sinead explains to her mother: 'She likes to experience the boredom. She doesn't want to read or talk or listen to music — it's to see how long she can last just doing nothing.'

Clara clearly thinks it's marvellous. 'You're meditating, darling,' she says to Zoe. 'Do you know what meditation is?'

Of course she does. Zoe's best friend has an uncle who is a Buddhist. 'He meditates. He says that if you can interrupt someone when they are meditating then they aren't meditating.'

'Then you weren't meditating.' Sinead laughs.

Zoe just rolls her eyes and turns back to the window. 'I never said I was.'

As they leave the highway and drive into the national park surrounding Bundeena, the change is dramatic. They are the only car now, and out the window there is nothing but bush: blue-grey eucalypts, sandy scrub, delicate ferns, gnarled bottlebrush, and the last remaining stalks of

Gymea lilies piercing the sky. The road narrows, twisting up and down hills, pressing in close to the rocky outcrops that delineate the roll of the landscape.

'It's beautiful, isn't it?' Sinead opens her window, breathing in the sharp air. She wants her mother to also appreciate the beauty, to show how much she, too, loves it. 'And so close to the city. That's what's incredible. Less than an hour and you're here.' She needs Clara for her plan to work. She could take out a lease with friends, but if she has Clara on board, it's one less person she will have to find, and she and her mother will have some flexibility in any timeshare arrangement they establish. It is the perfect way to have a holiday house, she thinks, visualising weekends swimming, relaxing in the garden, and having friends to stay.

But as they turn into Bundeena, she finds herself disappointed. Just slightly. And as the disappointment descends, she is aware that this is how she usually feels when she comes here. It is more suburban than she wants it to be. There are brick veneer houses with huge extensions, and a new development on the main street, the construction noisy, the scaffolding high enough to threaten something substantial. But she says nothing.

'It's a perfect day for an ice-cream,' she tells Zoe.

'Magnum?' Zoe immediately seizes on the offer.

'I don't know about that,' Sinead says. 'We'll look at the houses, have lunch, maybe a swim and then decide.'

'Bloody hell. Do we have to do all that first?'

Clara frowns as she opens the door to the noise of the construction. Her chiffon scarves float, flimsy in the stiff sea breeze. 'I do wish you wouldn't say "bloody",' she says.

Sinead grins. 'Oh, for god's sake. There are far worse things she could say.'

'Well, I don't like it.'

'So how many bloody houses are we going to see?' Zoe asks.

'Four,' Sinead tells her as they walk up a set of stairs.

'Bloody hell. We'd better start then or we'll be here all day.'

Clara pointedly ignores her, concentrating instead on the pictures of properties for sale outside the real estate agent's office. She taps on the glass, and the agent recognises her and waves.

'Kevin.' She greets him enthusiastically and introduces him to Sinead and Zoe.

'So, which ones are we interested in today?' he asks, and Clara runs through the list of shacks for sale.

'But first we want to inspect the rental houses,' Sinead adds, handing him her own list before frowning at Zoe, who is flicking stones at car tyres. Clara's dog hangs its head out the window, a sticky thread of saliva running from its teeth down the glass.

'Pepper,' Zoe calls to her, and she barks. 'Pepper,' she calls again, and the dog barks a little louder.

Across the road a group of teenage girls walk down towards the ferry. Their clothes are too tight, their skirts too short. One has a T-shirt with *Sex kitten* written in hot pink across her breasts; another has *Foxy* across her backside. Zoe watches them, and exchanges a look with Sinead.

Girlie girls, she mouths.

Sinead nods, the sight of the teenagers only deepening her sense of disappointment. Joining Zoe by the car, she glances up the street at the supermarket and bottle shop and across to the construction site, before finally turning to the sliver of blue water at the end of the road.

With a map clutched in one hand (in case they lose Kevin en route), Clara makes her way down the stairs towards them. She holds on to the railing, and places one foot carefully in front of the other. It has only been three weeks since her operation, and she has recovered remarkably well. In another three weeks, she will start the chemotherapy, and Sinead knows this will be hard. She has seen Clara's friends go through similar treatments and how ill they have become.

When the cancer was first diagnosed, Sinead went with her mother to the surgeon's rooms, ready to take notes.

'I won't remember anything,' Clara had said, and Sinead had promised she would be there, keeping a record of all he said.

The doctor's office was high above street level. Sinead could see out across the city, awash with rain, trees sodden and swaying in the wind. In front of her, the surgeon turned his pen, point down, point up, over and over again, as he listened to Clara tell him *how she understood the situation to be.*

When she finished by saying that she hoped it would just be a lumpectomy and not a mastectomy, he became impatient.

'You have been reading too many *Women's Weeklys*,' he said. 'There is no such thing as a lumpectomy. What we do,' and he drew a breast on the paper in front of him, 'is take a slice of the pie.' He outlined a triangle in the corner of the breast. 'We need to get out the cherry, but to do so we have to take an entire piece of the pie.' He pushed the paper across the desk, and Clara pushed it back to him.

The surgeon ignored it. He reached for his file and told her he needed to ask her a few questions.

'Medication?'

Clara listed them all: blood pressure, HRT, Epilum and antidepressants. Sinead had no idea about the last one. She glanced sideways at her mother.

'Menstruation?'

'Not for years.' Clara sounded surprised.

That was not what he'd meant. When did she begin? he asked.

'When I was about thirteen.'

'And stop?'

'Late forties.'

'Pregnancies?' The doctor scrawled notes without looking up.

'Four.' Clara hesitated. 'Well, two I carried to full term. And two I terminated.'

Again, Sinead hadn't known.

'Breastfeed?'

'No,' Clara told him.

He wanted to clarify the names of each of the medications she was on, and Clara searched for where she had written the information.

'You can email me,' the surgeon said, as she covered his desk with scraps of paper.

Shamefaced, she gathered them together, crushing them into her bag.

'Now let me explain,' he sat back in his chair, head resting against the leather, 'the exact procedure.'

This was when Sinead was expected to start writing, and she opened her book and waited, pen in hand.

'Ah, the little scribe.' The doctor turned to her. His eyes were amused. 'Shall I speak slowly?'

She stared back at him. 'We'll tell you when we need you to slow down.'

'It's important that you listen to me, and to me alone. I don't want you reading those women's magazines, or going on Google or talking to your friends. You would be amazed at the misinformation people manage to latch on to, vulnerable people, vulnerable women, in particular.'

'And who else, may I ask, do you see other than vulnerable women?' Clara rose in her chair. She had been a beauty once, strong, fine-featured, with a patrician nose and dark eyes. Beneath the smudged make-up, caked powder and those endless chiffon scarves that were always slightly grubby at the edges, there was a glimpse of her old dignity. Sinead reached across and took her mother's hand, but Clara brushed her aside and stood.

'This is not going to work,' she told the doctor. 'Thank you for your time.' The shake in her voice was barely evident.

Following her mother's lead, Sinead also got up, nodding hastily at the doctor before she, too, turned to the door.

Outside the surgery, they walked quickly, and silently, to the lift. It was only when the elevator doors closed that Sinead finally spoke. He was a pig. She was so proud of Clara. How dare he treat her like that?

'Oh god,' Clara said. 'I left my X-rays in there. I need them.'

She wanted Sinead to go up and get them for her.

'I need them.' She was panicked now. 'I'm going to have to find someone else and get this out.' She touched her breast. 'And I don't want to waste time messing around with getting the scans from one person to the next.'

The doctor was in the reception area when Sinead returned. Neither of them acknowledged the other. Hating herself for blushing, Sinead reached across the desk and whispered her request to the woman who answered the phones. Without a word, the surgeon handed the envelope to her, nodding at his next patient as he did so.

Downstairs, Clara was sitting on a vinyl bench by the elevator. Her whole body had shrunk, her scarves were tangled around her neck, and her make-up formed a dark circle around her left eye. She looked as old and as ill as she was.

'I've got them,' Sinead reassured her, holding up the X-rays.

Clara didn't even seem to notice. 'You would think that all my years as an active feminist, a woman who had a seat in parliament as an independent, all of that ...' She waved her arm and then let it fall to her side. 'You would think I would have found it easy to tell him where to get off.'

'At least you did it,' Sinead said, and she led her mother slowly towards the carpark.

The first house they inspect is the cheapest place for rent. It's an old fibro shack on the corner of a busy street, with a lantana-choked garden that drops away down the side of a cliff. A Moreton Bay fig obscures any light, and the recent rains have caused fat fingers of mildew to creep up the walls.

Kevin tries the key and then kicks the door open, stepping over a moth-eaten blanket on the worn linoleum. 'The very best in security.' He laughs. 'A lick of paint, bit of furniture, and who knows what you'll have.'

'I like it,' Clara says.

Sinead rolls her eyes. 'No, you don't.'

'I do, actually.'

There are holes in the walls, and two of the windows are smashed. The rooms are dark and cramped, and the garden is unusable. Sinead points all this out to Clara. Zoe, who has been outside with Pepper, stands at the front door, takes one look, and tells them both it's a bloody dump.

'Well, I think it has charm,' Clara insists.

They drive straight past two of the other places after Clara pronounces them 'suburban', and by the time they get to the fourth, which is opposite the RSL, Sinead is ready to give up. She winds down the window to let Kevin know that they won't bother with this one either, but Clara stops her. She wants to go inside.

'Why?' Sinead says. 'You'd hate the noise.' She points at the club opposite.

'No, I wouldn't.'

'I'll stay in the car,' Zoe informs them.

Inside, the shack is in slightly better condition than the first place they saw. But there is, at least, light in the rooms, and the windows around the sunroom are the old wooden ones that slide open to let in the sea breeze. Out the back the lawn is freshly mowed, and there is a rusted Hills hoist that squeaks as it turns. Perhaps, Sinead thinks, they could have a table out here, people for lunch? She knows she is stretching the possibilities to a point that may not have much grounding in reality, but it is better to cling to some hope than to completely give up.

In the kitchen, Clara is telling Kevin that she is planning on using this or some other place as a retreat. 'A bolthole where I can write my memoirs,' she says. 'And a way of deciding if I ultimately want to buy down here.'

'Well, it's yours if you want it.'

'I propose we have some lunch and a think,' Clara announces. 'We might also drive ourselves around and have a look at the outside of the houses for sale.'

She seems tired now. It happens quickly, a sudden fading in her eyes, a drop in her shoulders, a certain slowness in her speech, and she needs to rest.

'About bloody time,' Zoe says, when they eventually give up on finding the last of the places on Clara's list and pull up outside the café in the main street. 'I'm starving.'

There is a chill in the air, but they take an outside table so they can keep an eye on Pepper, who is tied up and barking.

'She'll quieten down soon.' Clara sits back in the chair and closes her eyes. 'Just ignore her.'

Zoe wants a hamburger — 'not the kid's size, the grown-up one' — and a banana smoothie.

'If you have the smoothie, then you can't have an ice-cream,' Sinead says.

'Bloody hell.' The agony of the choice makes Zoe frown. 'What about a small smoothie and a cheap ice-cream, like a Paddle Pop?'

'One or the other.'

'But that's not fair: you said I could have an ice-cream.'

'If you don't stop the bloody whining, you'll have nothing.'

Zoe glowers.

'I'll get you an ice-cream, darling,' Clara tells her. 'If you stop saying "bloody".'

Sinead begins to argue and then can't be bothered.

Zoe promises, most definitely, that she won't utter another 'bloody'. 'Can you get me a Magnum?'

At this point Sinead says she's going inside to order — she's had enough of both of them. 'You're bloody awful, the pair of you.'

'Don't forget I want a large burger,' Zoe calls out. 'And a smoothie.'

Two weeks after Clara came out of hospital, her closest friend, Kathryn, died. She, too, had breast cancer, the cancer recurring three years after she had finished her treatment.

At the funeral, Sinead sobbed. She began as soon as she sat down, unable to stop as each person spoke, and continued after the service had finished and family and friends gathered out the front of the church. She knew she had to go and speak to Sean, Kathryn's son, and she tried to get her tears under control.

Clara was laughing with one of Kathryn's other friends, and rubbed at the edge of her eyes as she put her sunglasses back on.

That was a lovely service, Sinead wanted to say to Sean, but she managed no more than the first two words before she began sobbing again. 'I am so sorry,' she said when she could finally speak. 'This is so inappropriate.'

She could see he didn't know how to respond. He had always been uncomfortable with her since they had sex, once, when they were both seventeen. For a brief period afterwards, Sinead thought she was madly in love with him, while he was quite certain that it had been no more than a very bad mistake. Now they rarely saw each other, and she never thought of him, although Clara had always kept her up to date with his news — a marriage, children, partnership in an accounting firm, an affair, a divorce. He probably knew about her as well — her relationship with Luka, Zoe's birth, and their separation when she had decided that she was perhaps more interested in women.

'It was a lovely service.' Sinead tried to sound like she was, in fact, okay now, it had just been a minor aberration, and then, as she began to cry once more, Clara came over and took her by the arm.

'I'll miss her,' Clara told Sean, and she kissed him on the cheeks.

In the car Sinead blew her nose several times, scrunching the last sodden tissue into a ball before dropping it onto the floor.

'I'm not dead yet,' Clara eventually said.

Sinead took a deep breath. She looked at herself in the

rear-vision mirror: her nose was red, her eyelids swollen and sore, her mascara had run, and she had a piece of food from breakfast still wedged between her two front teeth. 'What a mess.'

Clara reached out and put her hand on Sinead's knee. Sinead rested her own hand on top, the first few liver spots forming on her skin and dried purple ink crusted around her fingernails. She thought she had washed it all off when she had finished teaching her printmaking class last night.

'Shall we go to the wake?' She turned to her mother, who nodded, taking out a fresh tissue.

'But clean yourself up first, darling,' and Clara spat on it, wiping Sinead's face, before she could stop her.

When lunch is served, Sinead and Clara both wish they'd ordered a burger and smoothie, rather than lentil patties and herbal tea.

'Don't drink it all,' Zoe says, arm outstretched to take the glass back as Sinead takes a sip.

'It is hers,' Clara adds as Sinead keeps drinking.

'It's enormous,' Sinead tells them both. 'And I paid for it.'

Clara has a piece of paper in front of her and she is jotting down figures.

'We can do the first house or the last,' she says. 'But it means no trip to Europe.'

Shortly after she was diagnosed with cancer, she had

told Sinead and Zoe she wanted to take them both to Italy. Why not spend the money before she died, she said. Why not have fun? Sinead had been furious. It wasn't practical to organise a trip now. They didn't know how the operation would go, and how she would feel after the follow-up treatment. They were sitting in the kitchen at Sinead's house, the night warm, the cicadas throbbing outside. Zoe had the television turned up so she could hear her program, but she had come in at the mention of overseas travel.

'Can we go? Can we go?' She jumped up and down, short sharp bounces that rattled the table and all the plates and glasses on it.

'I don't see why not,' Clara had replied, pouring herself a third glass of wine. 'But then you and I have adventurous spirits, my darling.' She took Zoe's hand in her own. 'We are alike.'

After dinner Sinead had told her it was all very well to play a little 'let's go to Europe' game with her, but not with Zoe. 'You could see how excited she was. And you're only going to let her down.'

Why not be optimistic, Clara had insisted. They could book for six months after the end of her treatment and if she couldn't go then, well, so what? The worst that could happen was that she might lose some money on the tickets.

'No,' Sinead replied. 'The worst that could happen is that you might be dead.'

The trip wasn't mentioned again. Not until now, and Sinead pushes her plate away, leaving the last of the barely edible lentil patties untouched.

'I'd rather go to Europe than rent a bloody dump,' Zoe says, and realising her error, she grins. 'Correction: a nasty dump.'

Sinead is silent.

'Well, let's face it,' Clara says. 'If we're assuming I'm going to be well enough to come for weekends away down here, we might as well assume I'll be able to travel to Italy.'

There is quite a difference between an hour's drive down the coast and a twenty-four-hour plane flight, Sinead reminds her.

'All I'm saying is it's one or the other.' Clara raises her hand, trying to catch the attention of a passing waitress. 'I can't afford both.'

Later, Sinead swims out into the bay. The water is cool with the first autumn tides, but as she takes strong strokes forward she begins to feel the warmth of her blood, coursing throughout her body.

Behind her, Zoe is holding on to a kickboard, making her own way a little to the left, while back on the beach, Clara dozes against a rock with Pepper beside her, her head tilted up to the afternoon sun, her eyes closed.

It is almost empty. Midweek, end of summer, and only a father and his son sit on the sand. In the distance, a woman in pink tracksuit pants jogs to the other end, her dog following her, chasing the stick she throws out into the ocean for him. Sinead lets herself float into shore.

It is a beautiful beach, she thinks, grateful that this, at least, hasn't disappointed her, and that she can still hope she might one day rent a shack down here, a place to get away and do some of her own work, have friends to stay. As the sea becomes shallow, she stands, looking up to where Zoe is jumping on the sand, agitated.

'There are sea lice,' she calls out, and it's true, Sinead is also starting to feel itchy.

They grab their towels and rub them over their skin until the sting begins to ease.

'I'm not going in again,' Zoe says.

Sinead walks to the water's edge. A cob of corn washes against her feet, and she steps back, irritated. It is the father and his son. They are tossing them out to sea as soon as they finish eating them, the gnawed ends floating straight back.

'It's disgusting,' she tells Clara in a loud voice.

'Sshh,' Zoe urges, embarrassed.

'I want them to hear,' Sinead says.

'Well, why don't you just tell them directly?' Clara tries to lift herself up, holding on to the rock behind her as she pulls her body onto her knees and then into a standing position.

Sinead helps her. 'Because I'm too pathetic,' she confesses.

'I'm a little like that myself,' Clara says.

The woman in the pink tracksuit walks past them, raising a hand in greeting. They watch her head over the rocks and up to one of the larger brick houses built right on the water's edge.

'I'll probably never go jogging again.' Clara sighs.

'You never did go jogging.' Sinead gathers their towels and tells Zoe to take the kickboard and Pepper. 'Shall we just head home?' she asks, and Clara nods.

They walk back up the path to the car, Sinead leading the way, Zoe following, and Clara taking her time. Out on the street, they pass one of the original shacks, the paint peeling and the garden overgrown with grevillea and bottlebrush. Sinead turns back to Clara, who has also paused to peer into the yard.

'Now that's what I like,' Clara says. 'If that one was for sale —' She catches her breath before she continues to where Sinead and Zoe brush the sand from their legs and arms, ready to pull their clothes over their still-damp swimmers.

It is later than they thought, the clarity of the day softening into the cool of afternoon more quickly now that summer is ending. But despite the chill, Zoe still wants to stop for an ice-cream.

At the local shop, Sinead buys three Magnums, knowing they will not go to the agent's and fill out a rental form for any of the houses, nor will they look at the last of the places for sale. Instead, they will head out through the national park and back onto the highway that leads into the city, talking about how they might come back to see the last place again ('not the first — it was a dump,' Sinead will insist, and Clara will continue to disagree), while in the back seat, Zoe will sit, cheek against the window, wanting to experience only the boredom the whole way home.

Flyover

Sometimes, as I wait in a line of traffic near the turn-off to Glebe, I glance up to the three apartment blocks pressed tight against the tangle of roads. I wonder which of the windows in which of these buildings looks out from the room where I once spent the night with a man I didn't know. I have no idea, although I think perhaps he was living in the first block, the one closest to the flyover.

I had just turned nineteen when I stayed with him. Sydney was new to me, and I had no work, little money and only two friends, both of whom had come from Adelaide as well. Each Friday night we went to a bar that had once been a funeral parlour. Upstairs the music was a deep thud in the smoky darkness, while downstairs it was quieter, and you could sit in armchairs and drink.

He was the barman.

He was certain he knew me, or so he said the first time he took my order. He leant across the counter, his black fringe falling over his eyes, his skin pale in the blue light from the mirrors behind him. He had given us double shots, he told me, and I could taste the bitter gin before I even had a sip, the inside of my mouth dry with the memory of what was to come.

The next time, he asked me what I did, and I said I was trying to find a job.

'Modelling? Acting?' He slid the money I was offering back towards me, one hand still on top of it.

I said that I wanted to be a journalist, ignoring the notes he had pushed across the counter.

Cate was bemused by my refusal. 'It's not like we don't need it.' She examined him, eyes narrowed. 'Not bad-looking,' she decided. 'But not my type.'

She was the only one of us who had a job. As a production assistant on a television show, her wage wasn't high, but she was earning, and had hopes of a rapid ascent to something better. Loene and I were staying on the floor of the house she was minding until the end of the month, nibbling away at the edges of our savings, anxious about each dollar we spent.

And so I ordered for us again.

'Where do you live?' His fingers rested on the damp cardboard coaster, as he tilted his head to flick his hair out of his eyes. He shrugged away my offer of payment, and this time I accepted.

We were looking for a place, I said. I reached for the drinks, unable to avoid touching his hand, his skin clammy.

He told me I reminded him of someone. 'An actor.'

'That's so corny,' and I shook my head in embarrassment.

'Want to do something when I finish my shift?' His hand was on my arm. 'It's only an hour away.'

I said I was busy, despite knowing it would soon be obvious I had no plans other than staying here and getting drunk.

'I won't give up,' he told me.

And he didn't: the next Friday he asked me out again.

'I have Tuesday nights off.' He held his hands in prayer position.

It had been a bad week. I had been called in by a magazine, only to be told by the editor that she had asked to see me not because she had work for me, but simply to give me some advice.

'You're wasting your time sending a CV like this around.' She tapped my neatly typed pages with the tip of a long crimson fingernail. 'You have no experience. None at all. Your whole approach is wrong. The way to get into this industry is either contacts, or you start at the bottom of a down-market publication.'

She was right. It had been a waste of time. Worse, she had succeeded in making me feel small, but I thanked her for trying to help me.

'I could take you out for a meal,' the barman pleaded. 'At least give me your number.'

I could see the back of his head reflected in the mirror, obscuring my own face. In the dim lighting, my arms appeared to come from his body, and I smiled.

'That's a yes?'

What would it hurt? It wasn't like my life was particularly good as it was. I took the pen he gave me and wrote my name and number on the back of the coaster, the ink barely legible as it bled into the damp.

A few weeks ago, when I was waiting in the airport lounge for the plane back to Sydney, I thought I saw him again. I don't remember much about him — the exact location of his flat, his name, and the finer details of how he looked are all gone. There is only a vague sense of his dark hair and the white of his skin. But as I sat there with my work files unopened on the table in front of me, a plate of wilted salad on my lap, I found myself staring at a man two seats to my left. He glanced up, and I glanced away. Seconds later, he caught me staring at him again.

Embarrassed, I half acknowledged him. He turned back to his magazine. He was pale and slightly overweight, his shirt stretched a little too tight around his waist, his hair still falling foppishly across his forehead.

The announcement for the flight echoed through the lounge, and I stood, forgetting the salad on my lap. The plate slid onto the carpet, the contents leaving an oily stain as I tried to pick up the mess.

I was one of the last on board, and in the cramped aisle I waited for another passenger to force her bag into the overhead locker. When I finally got to my seat, I saw that he was sitting by the window.

I apologised while trying to extract my seatbelt from the gap between us. As he shifted his weight, I noticed the softness of his hands, a single gold band around his wedding-ring finger.

I was forced to tug the belt out from underneath him and our eyes met. I wanted to say then that I was sorry for having stared at him in the lounge, and that I wasn't sure if I knew him. The thought, however, of opening up what could be an awkward conversation, with no escape for the next hour, kept me silent; instead, I took the magazine out from the seat pocket and flicked through articles I had read on the way down a week earlier.

I had been covering a conference on global warming, filing stories on a regular basis and working on a feature for the weekend edition. As an industrial reporter, this was not a job I would normally have taken, but in the last month Jason had decided to return to his wife and children. It was a decision we had discussed for some time, moving from a bleak awareness that his wife's illness meant this could be necessary, to realising that this was, in fact, the inevitable place to which we had come. At first we had talked constantly, picking over and over the decision until, weighed down by the inadequacy of words, we had pared back all discussion to the cold practicalities. This was the week he was going to pack and organise a truck to clear out all he owned from our house. It would be easier if I wasn't there and he could just get the job done.

Now, at the end of what had been a busy five days, I was bracing myself for the return to Sydney. Ultimately I would be alright. But there was first the space between now and a time, somewhere in the future, when we would have either let each other go, or negotiated some form of friendship. That was what made me anxious.

Once again, I glanced briefly at the man next to me, wanting to distract myself from the thought of my homecoming. I was careful to keep my head lowered and my eye contact barely noticeable. He was gazing out the window at the tufts of cloud that wrapped us, grey and insubstantial, drifting like floss around the plane. I wished I could remember his name but I couldn't, and I knew I had no hope of guessing what it might be. Nothing out of the ordinary, that was all I could recall. Robert, perhaps? His hands were resting in his lap, fingers curled tight into the palm. As he turned, I glanced away, careful not to be caught out again.

Robert, and I will call him that because it is a name as good as any other, phoned me the morning after I gave him my number. I had woken, my sheets pulled back to reveal the bare mattress on the floor. The lounge room where I slept still smelt of cigarette smoke and the cheap perfume we'd put on before heading out the previous night. Through the gap in the curtains I could glimpse a sliver of sharp light that hurt my eyes.

When I first decided to move to Sydney, I thought I would find work almost immediately. I saw myself in my own house. I envisaged friends. Lately I wanted to go home, back to South Australia, but this never developed beyond a general desire to return because there was, in reality, no family house to go back to, no work there, just a few friends who would welcome me but would probably not shift or adjust their lives to fit me back within the fold. I had my sister, who lived with her husband and children in the foothills. They went to our church each week, and spoke a language I had never understood, one of Christ and heaven and hell, and absolute rights and wrongs. My mother was in the granny flat at the back of their house, although she would soon have to go to a home. Sometimes she knew who we were, sometimes she didn't. She sat in the lounge room and called the grandchildren over to sit on her lap, making up different names each time and wondering why they never answered. She was only sixty, but she seemed so much older.

Next to me, Loene stirred, snorting as she rolled to one side, her hand flung out onto the floor; while upstairs Cate slept in the one bedroom, a narrow white chamber with a broken window that looked over the back lane.

In the courtyard, I sat on the step and drank a cup of tea, staring at the gate, loose on its hinges from drunks and junkies trying to break in.

We were meant to be inspecting a house for rent in less than an hour, and I knew I should wake the others, but I wanted to shower first, ensuring that I got some of the hot water. I tiptoed into the lounge, careful not to trip over the mattress, lurching for the phone as it rang.

Robert — he is becoming that name as I use it more frequently — wanted to meet me at a café in Glebe. I wrote the address down on a scrap of paper, although I knew the place he suggested.

'What are you up to today?' he asked.

I told him we were house-hunting. 'It's what we always do,' I said.

'Whereabouts?'

'Darlinghurst, Newtown, Glebe.'

He wished me luck. He said he was looking forward to seeing me. 'Tuesday,' he reminded me. 'Seven o'clock.'

I hung up and crumpled the paper in my hand.

'Who was that?' Loene wanted to know, and I blushed as I admitted it was the barman. But she didn't wait to hear my reply. She had pushed past me, closing and locking the bathroom door behind her before I had time to protest.

When I arrived the following Tuesday, he was already at a table. I could see him through the window, and I only wanted to walk away and go home, but I stood there watching him turn the menu over and over, the plastic coating slipping between his fingers. He saw me and stood, beckoning me inside.

The café was crowded, and I had to squeeze past other tables to get to where he waited for me in the corner. As he tried to kiss me on the cheek, I pulled back, but he held my hand firmly, drawing me close.

'How is it all going? The house-hunting? The job search?' There was a wetness to his lips that I noticed as he slurped the soup from his spoon, leaving a fine coating of liquid over the metal.

I shouldn't have come. This, too, was not going to be what I had tried to fool myself into thinking was possible. I had never liked him in the bar, and being alone with him in a café hadn't changed that. But still I continued to try, hoping that, at some stage in our conversation, a magical transformation would occur, lifting the veil to reveal a man whom I could find attractive.

When I told him I had had no luck with either, he sat back in his chair and wiped at his mouth with a paper serviette.

'Perhaps I could help with one,' he said.

I didn't see how.

'I was the personal assistant to the editor-in-chief of *The Australian*. I could introduce you or, at the very least, give him your CV.'

Why, I thought, had he gone from a job like that to working in a bar? Even if he was telling me the truth, an introduction or a CV into the right person's hands wouldn't be enough. I had no experience. Not even volunteer or student work to suggest that I could possibly be a journalist. It was hopeless, I told him.

'You can't think like that. Let me help,' he said.

'Sure,' I replied, wanting only to end such a foolish conversation.

He ordered dessert. A cake to share, he suggested, and despite my saying I wasn't hungry, he asked the waiter for two forks.

'When I first came to Sydney, I knew no one,' he said. 'It can be a lonely place. I'd like to take you out. I know all the clubs. I can show you some fun.'

He named a few places I had heard of, and I told him I wasn't into clubs.

'I'm not a good dancer,' I said.

'What about the theatre?'

I didn't like plays.

I was making it hard, he said, and I knew I was. Each time he tried to prise the door open a little I would pull it closed, unable to bear the thought of letting him in. Now, I wonder at my cruelty, but at the time I thought my behaviour was justified. He was too cocky, too smooth, and therefore not worthy of more gentle consideration.

At the end of our meal, he offered to pay, and I let him.

'Shall we go somewhere else?' he said.

We stood outside the café, people walking past us on

the pavement, cars slowing down in search of a park, the faint sound of music coming from the record shop two doors down. Across the road from us, a couple argued, her in the car, him still on the road. She slammed the door on him, and he kicked at the bumper bar. Moments later, Robert asked me if I wanted to come home with him, the directness of his request throwing me off balance.

So, it has come to this, I thought, both surprised that he could think it was possible I would agree and yet also aware that this was, of course, the inevitable conclusion of our evening out. He wanted to have sex with me.

'I'm not so sure,' I tried to say, but my protest was feeble. If this was the place to which we had been headed, I might as well just give in and go there. Perhaps sex would finally bring the transformation I seemed to want to continue believing was possible, despite all evidence to the contrary.

He had parked his car, a dented old Toyota, in a side street. He cleared papers and cigarette packs and a jumper off the front seat before opening the passenger door for me, his body still stretched across the driver's seat as I sat down, his hand touching my leg. And then he opened his window to the night air as we drove, in silence, towards the apartment blocks that line what has now become a tangle of roads.

A few weeks ago, as I sat on the plane next to the man who I thought was Robert, I wondered at how lonely I had once been. I found it hard to recall the feeling. Even in the last few months, as it became clear to me that Jason needed to go back to his wife and that I was going to have to let him go with grace, I never felt the complete cold emptiness I had experienced in those early days of living in Sydney.

Robert was still staring out of the curved window, arms crossed, and as I stole a glance at him I wanted to dispel the shame of remembering the girl I used to be. It was then that the plane shuddered, suddenly losing altitude. In the aisle, the flight attendant tried to steady the drinks trolley. Her face was turned away from me, but there was no visible change in her posture, no reason to feel panic, and I leant back in my seat. After a few seconds the plane dropped again, and the captain asked all passengers and crew to return to their seats as further turbulence was expected.

Robert was staring directly at me.

In the dim light of the cabin it was, at first, difficult to tell if there was panic in his eyes. But when the captain announced that the plane would need to return to Canberra, his anxiety was unmistakable.

'I'm terrified of flying.' He grimaced.

'Ladies and gentlemen' — the flight attendant's voice was calm — 'the captain informs me that there has been a minor technical fault, which unfortunately means we need to land at the closest airport. As we will be flying into some weather, we ask that you all remain seated until the plane has safely landed. We do apologise for any inconvenience.'

'It will be alright,' I told him.

But he wasn't listening. His pupils were glassy and his voice tight. He said he'd had a bad feeling from the minute he got on the plane. 'Did you hear that?'

I hadn't.

'The strain in the engine.'

I tried to ignore the panic that surged as we dropped altitude once more. Was this the end? It was impossible. In the back a woman screamed, followed by a man's nervous laughter.

The captain spoke now. 'Ladies and gentlemen, I do want to assure you that there's no reason for anxiety. As Damien mentioned to you earlier, we are simply experiencing some bad weather. Unfortunately, we're having to fly directly into it in order to return to Canberra to rectify what is a very minor fault with the back-up navigation system. It has no impact on our safety but it is something we are obliged to fix under aircraft laws and regulations. If I could just urge you all to stay seated and calm, we should have you landed within the next twenty minutes.'

'It's worth trying to believe him.' I kept my voice level, trying to convince both myself and Robert. 'Doubting won't help any of us.' My hand gripped the armrest, and I could taste the acid fear at the back of my mouth.

Robert was white, and his pupils had flooded, black,

into the dark of his eyes.

I asked him if he lived in Canberra or Sydney, and he told me neither.

'Melbourne,' he said, voice soft.

Behind us, I could hear other passengers talking. We were all trying to convince one another there was no need for alarm.

'Were you working in Canberra?'

Robert nodded. He was a lobbyist, for the music industry. He was there often.

'I usually drive,' he confessed.

'And Sydney?' I asked.

It was where most of his clients were based. 'And my son. He lives there with my first wife.'

The plane lurched again, and whatever calm had begun to still him dissipated. 'Are we going to be alright?' he asked, clutching the armrest between us.

'Of course we are.' I spoke quickly, not wanting to let my own fear in, but it was there, searing and raw as I laid my hand on top of his and held it tight.

Robert's apartment was like a cheap hotel room. He opened the front door and stepped back to let me in.

'Drink?'

I shook my head.

The plastic vertical blinds were drawn across the only window, but I could just make out a two-seater couch, a glass coffee table, and in the corner a large television. To our left was a galley kitchen, and on our right, a closed door that led, I presumed, to Robert's bedroom.

'I can't do this,' I suddenly said.

In the distance I could hear the faint rumble of traffic and, from somewhere along the corridor outside, the thud of a door as it closed.

'Of course you can.' Robert stepped close, the smell of his aftershave sweet, as he kissed me, his lips on mine.

Of course I could, I told myself.

As he began to undress me, thick fingers fumbling with my bra strap, I said I needed to go to the bathroom first.

Under the fluorescent light, I undressed myself, avoiding my reflection in the mirror. I gathered my clothes in a pile and walked to where he waited in the bedroom. He pulled back the cover and I got into the bed with him, the sheets cold beneath me.

'Wait,' I said as he moved towards me.

I unbuckled my watch, leaving it not on top of my pile of clothes but on the bedside table next to me.

Later, when I realised I had left it behind, I wondered why I had taken it off in the first place. I had no intention of spending the night there, and could have just kept it on my wrist. Habit, I suppose.

'You're not leaving?' Robert reached for me as I sat up only moments after we had sex. My legs were cold, and I almost relented.

'Tell me more about yourself,' he said.

'There's not much to tell,' I replied.

'Your family?'

'They are very religious.'

'And you're the black sheep?'

It wasn't that simple. I didn't follow their faith, but I wasn't an outcast.

I pulled my top on and tied my hair back as I told him I was going to head home.

'At least let me drive you,' he offered, but I declined.

'You know,' and he touched my arm, 'if you relaxed with me you might get to like me.'

In the dark, it was hard to read his expression, but there was a plea in his eyes.

'Can I call you?'

I explained I'd rather he didn't.

'I don't understand.'

I was surprised, thinking he must have sensed I had no desire or attraction for him. I was with him because I needed to take myself right to the hard centre of the loneliness, and I had used him for that purpose only. Surely he could see that? And having seen it, why would he want to know me?

Outside in the cold, he waited with me for a taxi. As I shivered, he tried to rub my arms. *Stop*, I wanted to tell him. *This is not how it is between us. There is no affection.* But I let him try to keep me warm; I even let him kiss me goodbye as I got into the taxi, sinking back into the seat, and closing my eyes.

The next evening, when he rang to tell me he had my watch, I had already decided to let it go.

'You can pick it up at the bar,' he suggested. 'Or I could meet you somewhere.'

I was standing in the hallway. Loene and Cate were both in the lounge room, drinking cheap champagne, and able to hear every word.

'Can you post it to me?' I asked him.

'You don't want to see me that much?'

I said I was sorry. 'It's just the way it is.'

He was silent for the first time.

I gave him my address.

Loene was laughing. She was drunk already. Cate was trying to decide which skirt suited her better. They turned the music up another notch, and I heard the pop of the cork as they opened the second bottle.

'I'll post it,' he said.

I thanked him.

'Well. I hope you have a nice life.'

Wincing slightly at the anger in his tone, I said I hoped he did, too, and I hung up, relieved to have come to an end in our dealings with each other.

Two days later, the watch turned up in the mail, wrapped in tissue, with no note or return address on the envelope.

When the captain told us we were ready to land, I finally let go of Robert's hand. I hadn't quite realised I was still holding it, until I felt the tension in his fingers ease a little, my own hand relaxing on his.

For the last fifteen minutes we had talked. Rather, I had asked him questions and he had answered. He had told me his son was ten years old. His marriage had come to an end because of differences that could not be repaired, and then, when he explained to me that he lived with someone now, in a marriage of sorts, 'although we can't get married', I began to wonder whether he was gay.

When I told him my name, he showed no recognition. I kept talking. I said I was a journalist and I mentioned where I worked. I gave him no details of my personal life. I didn't think he took in anything I said: his whole being was attuned to the immediate danger of our predicament. My own anxiety was only just under control.

In fact, I had suppressed my panic to such an extent that it wasn't until much later, as I lay on top of the quilted bedspread in the hotel near the airport, that I began to properly breathe again, slowly, deeply. I closed the brocade curtains on the Canberra night, and I switched off the main light, leaving only the bedside lamp on.

The room was old-fashioned, ordinary, decorated in a deep plum and cream. It was a twin share, and I had taken the bed closer to the door.

I had a bath and poured myself a straight scotch, wanting that burning warmth, before I picked up the telephone.

Jason was still at our house. I had guessed he might be, waiting for my return so that he could say goodbye.

I was alright, I assured him, because he had seen the news. From first reports, it appeared we had been in greater danger than the pilot or flight attendants had admitted, although it was still unclear as to what the problem had been.

I told him I had sat next to a man I thought I knew from years ago. 'He was terrified, and so I just talked to him, the whole way back. I kept wanting to ask whether it was him, but I never did.'

On the other end of the phone, Jason was silent.

'You know,' I said, 'there was a moment when I prayed. Just quietly, to myself. It was the prayer they used to say in our church when I was young. It was running through my head as I kept asking him inane questions about his life. I could still remember it, word for word.'

In the quiet of the hotel room, I began to cry.

'I'm okay,' I assured him. 'It's just a delayed reaction. I distracted myself, the whole time, talking to that man, but I guess I was scared as well.'

He tried to comfort me, cutting in over the rapid flow of my words as I kept insisting I was fine, never giving him the space to say what I knew he wanted to say. He would miss me. I would miss him also, but this would lessen. The facts were such that we had no choice.

His wife's degeneration had been rapid. Soon she would be incapable of caring for herself, let alone the children. He was going back to her because he was a good man, and I was relinquishing, trying to cut loose all the threads that had linked and tied us for the past two years, because I, too, wanted to be decent. Older now, we had realised the importance of trying to behave like adults, even when we wanted nothing more than to cry out like a child.

Acknowledgements

Thanks to Ian See and Aviva Tuffield at Scribe for their meticulous editing. It was a joy to be in such good hands.

With love, as always, to Andrew and Odessa, and in memory of Harry, the dog, who seemed to creep into my stories with as much stealth as he crept onto the couch.